DANA SCHWARTZ

AND WE'RE OFF

RAZORBILL

An Imprint of Penguin Random House

RAZORBILL®

An Imprint of Penguin Random House LLC
Penguin.com

RAZORBILL & colophon is a registered trademark of Penguin Random House LLC

First published in the United States of America by Razorbill,
an imprint of Penguin Random House LLC, 2017

LIBRARY OF CONGRESS CATALOGING-IN-PUBLICATION DATA IS AVAILABLE
Hardcover ISBN: 9780448493817
Paperback ISBN: 9780448493824

Printed in the United States of America

1 3 5 7 9 10 8 6 4 2

Design: Eric Ford

For my mom,
who is only a tiny bit like Alice Parker.

I love you.

"I was supposed to be having the time of my life."
—Sylvia Plath, *The Bell Jar*

1

STOP IT, NORA. *You have more self-control than this.*

My fingers twitch on the keyboard, but my eyes don't move from the screen. It's not even that Nick's Facebook profile is *that* interesting. It's just . . . he changed his profile picture. Now, instead of the soccer team photo, he's posted a picture of him at a party, mid-laugh, looking away from the camera. His hair is wavy, almost wet-looking. In the corner of the picture is an arm that I know has to be Lena's because—

Stop it. I slam my laptop shut, like I'm actually closing my mind to all things Nick DiBasilio, and I make the responsible, adult decision to turn my attention to something slightly less sexy than the second alternate goalie on the boys' varsity soccer team: the drawing I'm working on of Harry Potter and Draco Malfoy making out. The sneer in Draco's upper lip isn't quite right. I need to make it clear from their body language alone: This isn't a truth-or-dare peck between Drarry—this is a full-blown kiss that's going to turn into some full-contact wand play in the Gryffindor common room later.

The gay erotic fandom community on Tumblr has turned out to be surprisingly profitable. Last month, I made enough money from customers—people requesting the most specific scenes they could think of—that I was able to go to Six Flags with Lena. For twenty dollars, I'll draw a cartoon of any two characters of your choosing. For thirty, I'll include a more elaborate background. And for fifty, I'll add you into the mix.

Today's to-do list includes the aforementioned gay Harry and Draco kiss ("No background, with Harry also wearing Slytherin robes too, please?") and one illustration of John Watson and Sherlock Holmes sharing a bathtub.

How long am I spending on the drawing? It could be ten minutes or ten years. My mind is so focused on perfecting that curl in Draco's lip, the slight . . . bulge . . . in his Hogwarts robe, making Harry's hair just messy enough, that by the time I finish the sun has gone down completely behind the white roof of the 7-Eleven outside my bedroom window.

I blow on the page, careful not to smudge any of the still-wet black ink, and set it carefully beside the letter that I've kept in the place of honor at the corner of my desk for two months.

The letter is written on gorgeous paper, cream-colored with a dark, pressed logo at the top of the page: a minimalist lighthouse. This is the type of letterhead Pinterest was born for, the kind of stationery porn that could launch a thousand BuzzFeed listicles.

And then my eyes sneak down the page, and it gets even better from there:

Congratulations! We are pleased to offer you a spot as one of eight fellows at the Donegal Colony for Young Artists in the summer of 2017.

I could recite the entire acceptance letter from memory, along with the rest of the welcome packet, which is filled with details about lodging and meals and travel tips. All of the shiny-haired, clear-skinned students featured in its glossy photographs look like they were caught in the middle of the most hilarious inside joke. The group of them—so casually diverse that they have to be staged—all have their heads tossed back in big Julia Roberts laughs. I practice opening and shutting my jaw, but I don't think I can even get my mouth that wide.

And then, a creak from the hallway tears me from my multiethnic reverie. I don't even need to look to know that my mother is standing in the doorway. I instinctually flip the packet shut and place it innocently atop my Drarry drawing (the ink must be dry by now, right?) before picking up another one of the commissioned pieces I recently finished—Hermione Granger reading in bed as a ten-year-old—and staring at it like I'm scanning for Egyptian hieroglyphs.

"You shouldn't be keeping this stuff," my mother says, walking into my room without being invited (there goes my theory that she's actually a vampire) and pawing through the pile of old sketchbooks and pages that have turned my desk into something of a paper Jenga game. I keep eyeing the drawing of Draco and Harry, worried that it might fly out from under the welcome packet of its own volition and show my mother exactly how intimate my knowledge of the cartoon male anatomy has become. "I swear," she says, "this room becomes messier every time I pass it. Are you *breeding* papers?"

"No, I'm pro-shelter."

She ignores my hilarious joke and continues surveying my room, her fingers playing with the chunky turquoise necklace that sits above her abomination of a coral-colored sweater. She was probably going for "Capable Mom Back in the Workforce!" but the effect is more "Middle-Aged *Little Mermaid* Cosplayer."

Her eyes settle on the green streak in my hair, which has been a topic in every single conversation we've had since I bleached and dyed it two weeks ago.

"It's like you've been using your hair as a Kleenex," she says, chuckling to herself with a clucking laugh like it's the funniest joke she ever heard.

"Do you mind?" I say. "I'm trying to work."

With a single stride, she crosses the room and snatches the Hermione drawing from my hand and brings it close to her face. "These aren't your applications," she says. "You're drawing cartoons, Nora. I mean, look at this." She lets the ripped, crumpled drawing fall to the floor. "You promised me you'd at least have a rough draft of your personal statement before you left."

I slide to the carpet to rescue the drawing, but the damage is done. Even after smoothing it out it, the wrinkles in the page mean I won't be able to upload the image. At least not without a spiderweb of shadow lines across it. A small tear threatens to separate Hermione's left leg from her torso.

"You ripped it!" I wave the ruined drawing in her face.

"Don't be so dramatic," she says.

"I'm not being dramatic!" I slam the drawing on top of the quivering tower of papers on my desk, and, with a sound like a cartoon *splat* effect, the entire stack comes tumbling down. Papers soar through the air and land all over my carpet.

Jenga.

"Ugh!" My mom jumps back from the swelling flood of papers as if she's trying to keep the hem of her pants dry. "Your room is a pigsty," she says, her gaze sweeping with disgust past the fallen pile of papers and toward the T-shirts and sweatpants that have settled into a nest on my bedroom floor. "When you leave, this is all going in the trash."

"This isn't trash! These are my drawings." I pull out a piece of scrap paper on which I doodled a giant man-eating pineapple with dripping fangs. "I mean, *most* of it isn't trash."

"I don't want to have to look at this."

"So don't. Just close my door and don't look. It's fine."

She clears her throat and repeats herself. "If I have to look at your messy room—"

"—which you *don't*."

"—which I *do* because it is in my home," she continues, straightening her already perfect-posture spine, "this is all going to be recycled."

"That's not fair. One, I need to pack. Also, don't forget Dad's wedding is tomorrow, and that means I won't have time to—"

My mother stiffens. I'm surprised she doesn't hiss like a vampire smelling garlic. She's mentioned Dad a grand total of three times since the divorce: once when he started dating Ms. Wright, once when she found his old navy-blue golf shirt in the wash (I was using it as a smock), and once when the wedding invitation arrived.

I didn't think it was biologically possible, but somehow, my mother's spine gets even straighter. "Clean your room, or I will deal with this when you're gone," she says and then leaves.

Since she's gone back to work, my mother has been stressed, but the past few weeks she's been criticizing my summer trip— three weeks at one of the most prestigious art programs for high school students *in the world*—as if it's a personal inconvenience. "I assume you'll be taking the money for airfare out of your Bat Mitzvah savings," she had said immediately after hearing I'd been accepted.

Grandpa understands, though. He knows what this opportunity means. He knows that listing the DCYA on my college applications is basically a golden ticket to the Rhode Island School of Design. He knows how long I spent agonizing over my application. *Should I include a landscape or an abstract portrait?* (I went with both in the end.) *What's the best way to ask my art teacher, Mr. Kall, for a recommendation? Will they even want an American there when, according to my research/stalking, they let in three Americans last year and their website says they want "diversity of nations among the admitted students"?*

I assume Grandpa pleaded my case to my mom, because two days later, despite continuing to mutter about "wasting time" and "focusing on a precollege program," she took me to get a passport. And when Grandpa broke the news that he was going to pay for me to travel around Europe before and after the weeks I would spend studying at the Donegal Colony in Ireland, she barely protested.

I begin cleaning up the papers from the floor: not just pineapple doodles, it turns out, but old English reports ("Red Light, Green Light: *The Great Gatsby* and American Industrialism"); several failed self-portraits created after spending hours studying my face in the mirror only to end up with a drawing that looked like Jar Jar Binks; a worksheet covered in calculus notes that don't look even a little bit familiar; and sketchbooks that I can't bring myself to throw away. Attempting to clean up now is akin to asking someone to drain the ocean with an eyedropper and be done by noon the next day: a futile effort. I let the pages fall from my arms back onto the floor and return to my desk to get a final look at the Drarry cartoon before I scan it to Tumblr. Let my mother yell about my messy room all she wants. I'll be across the Atlantic Ocean.

2

THE BARTENDER ISN'T paying any attention to me—that's the second problem with my night. I've fished out the fluorescent orange cherry from the bottom of my glass, and I've been swirling the stem back and forth between my cheeks, trying to tie it into a knot. I read somewhere that this is sexy, but even if I succeed, I still don't think it'll capture the bartender's attention. He's too busy wiping down wine glasses with a dust-gray rag to notice the not-completely-unattractive seventeen-year-old almost showing him how good she'd be at making out.

The first problem with my night is, obviously, that I'm leaving for Europe in two days and still haven't packed. And in an act of teenage anarchy that I'm not regretting in the slightest, I left my room covered in paper when I left for the wedding. Sure, it'll mean I'm facing a dual packing-and-scavenger-hunting endeavor when I return. But, you know: worth it.

And while I could be worrying about important things, like how I'm going to find my raincoat from underneath three semesters of essays (I still have a raincoat somewhere, right?) or my debilitating procrastination problem (will I be forced to tour Paris in a hotel towel because I forgot to bring enough underwear?), it's much more fun to focus exclusively on how I'm going to get the bartender to flirt with me.

He's cute in a brunette Ryan Gosling kind of way—if Ryan Gosling had a less-good-looking little brother who worked as a bartender and resented when strangers told him he kind of looks like that guy from *The Notebook*.

I probably shouldn't have ordered a Shirley Temple. If I had sidled up to the bar with confidence and a world-weary look in my eye that said, "Make it a double, pal," I bet he wouldn't have checked to see if I was twenty-one. Do they even card people at weddings? Probably not. Especially not if you're the groom's daughter. Especially not if you're the groom's daughter and the bride is your former math teacher. Sure, they didn't start dating until I was out of her class, but still, it's objectively weird. I had to deal with snide "PTA meeting" jokes for six months after Nick DiBasilio wrote something about it in the group text we had for homecoming plans that year. If the bartender knew about all of that, he'd definitely pour me a real drink.

I twist the green strand of hair around my finger. I was going for a chick-bassist look, the kind of casual just-woke-up-looking-this cool that you see on street style blogs where people look amazing in long T-shirts and hats that would make me look like a crazy lady at the beach. It seems like the purpose of street style blogs is to point out how incredibly attractive people still look incredibly attractive in strange clothes.

But here, in the yellow lighting of the Chicago Radisson ballroom, with a swelling red pimple on my nose threatening to overthrow the feeble ranks of Maybelline concealer, the green in my hair makes me look sickly. The ends of my hair are cracked and dry. I might have left the bleach on too long.

It's also worth noting that my dress—a taffeta nightmare that I've had sitting in the back of my closet since Bar and Bat Mitzvah season in seventh grade—is too tight. Even though I haven't gotten any taller since the last time I wore it, I still look totally wrong. I feel like an undercover policewoman dressing like a kid to bust a suburban high school drug ring.

"It's fine," my mother had told me when I came downstairs into the living room wearing it a few nights ago, trying to convince her to let me buy something new. Her fingers were absentmindedly circling a few kernels of popcorn at the bottom of her bowl, and she didn't even bother to look up from the latest episode of *Property Brothers* to see the way the fabric squeezed across my chest and stomach like a shiny sausage casing, outlining the shadow of my belly button. My mother also didn't notice the way I rolled my eyes and headed back upstairs, slamming my bedroom door behind me just to make good on the annoyed-teenager routine.

For whatever reason, the ponytailed wedding DJ (do all wedding DJs have ponytails?) thinks that people in the year 2017 still want to hear "The Chicken Dance." The song is quacking along when the DJ's voice comes through the speakers: "Let's welcome to the dance floor Mr. and Mrs. Holmes!"

My dad, Walter Holmes, who used to pick me up from soccer and tuck my stuffed elephant, Bobba, in bed next to me when I was little, is suddenly in the center of the dance floor flapping his arms and shaking his butt . . . *clap clap clap clap.*

I can't watch. I need the semi-cute bartender to save me, but he's still checking his cell phone and ignoring me. I abandon the cherry-stem plan (spitting it out as gracefully as I can into a monogrammed cocktail napkin), and I pick up a cardboard coaster from the artistically fanned stack in front of me. I place it, balanced, on the edge of the bar. With a quick flick of my wrist, I send the coaster into the air and catch it, one smooth motion before it even finishes its ascent.

It's a trick Grandpa taught me whenever I went with him to his country club. He'd walk into the clubhouse after a round of golf, and I'd already be waiting at the bar, swinging my legs on a stool, drinking a club soda through a straw, and plucking the cashews out of the plastic bowls of salted nuts. As we waited for our lunch to arrive, he'd flip one of the coasters and snatch it faster than I thought he was capable of moving. "Always impresses the ladies," he said, winking at the waitress in the clubhouse, the glint of his gold tooth deep in his mouth barely visible.

Just by looking at him, you'd have no idea that my grandpa is Great Living American Artist Robert Parker. With his taste for wrinkled khakis, sweater vests, and suspenders, he looks more like a retired middle school vice principal than the man who once sold a painting to George and Amal Clooney.

But even if people don't always recognize him by his appearance, they definitely recognize the look of his paintings, the style he's famous for—moments of tension, usually family scenes, frozen in time against a placid background.

The clubhouse had one of Grandpa's landscapes—not an especially famous one—hanging in a gold frame with a little light above it meant to illuminate the scene of the hill and the water mill. But that's not the painting that'd be an answer to a Daily Double on *Jeopardy!* or a question on the SAT:

Which of these is Great Living American Artist Robert Parker's most famous work?

A) *Nighthawks*
B) *American Gothic*
C) *The Reader and the Watcher*
D) *Water Lilies*

Ding ding ding! The correct answer is C, *The Reader and the Watcher*, that image of a living room with two figures, a young girl on a couch reading and a man by the window, looking out anxiously at something off the canvas. It's been praised for its ambiguity and tension. There have been at least two books written about what The Watcher is looking for: His wife? A lover? A mob boss after a drug deal went wrong? The distant promise of the American Dream? Most scholars have concluded that the stub of a still-burning cigarette in the figure's right hand represents class anxiety.

Seeing that painting was always the best part about taking class trips to the Art Institute of Chicago. Our teacher would announce that the painting was by Robert Parker, and then she'd pause, half-remembering some gossip from the art teacher or one of the other parents about someone in the class having a connection to the esteemed Chicago art figure, not quite confident enough about it to actually say anything. And then some kid would elbow me in the side and ask if it was by my dad, and I would say, a little louder than I needed to, "Actually, my grandpa." Cue the jealous glances and slack-jawed teacher.

Twice in elementary school, Grandpa came to my class to teach workshops, creating a fluster of superintendents, principals, and teachers all trying to make a good first impression.

"Let's use watercolors to paint the sky—darker at the bottom, lighter on the top," he'd say, flicking his wrists and rolling up his sleeves to paint an example, while we, a group of seven-year-olds with no idea how lucky we were to be getting an art lesson from *the* Robert Parker, would try to imitate his paper as best we could with our Crayola watercolor sets. While other kids drew the sun as a butter-yellow circle in the corner of the page, I knew, even then, that my landscape should have a clear source of light coming from off the page, illuminating the Tim Burton–round hills. Mine was always the painting that the other kids would pause behind and stare at when they crossed the classroom to get another brush.

"Runs in the family," a teacher would say with a knowing smile, and Grandpa would wink at me and dip his paintbrush again, like we were sharing a secret that no one else would ever understand.

Thankfully, "The Chicken Dance" ends, but the DJ replaces it with "YMCA," so it's hard to say whether there's any real improvement. Instead of watching the flailing, middle-aged upper arms jiggling on the dance floor, I keep flipping my coaster, trying to snatch it faster out of the air every time.

A little girl sees my trick from the dance floor and abandons her parents to run up to me at the bar. She barely reaches my boobs.

"Are you playing catch?" she asks. I don't recognize her—she must be on Ms. Wright's side of the family. (It's going to be weird to have to start calling her Tina.) Her purple dress already has an almost black streak of a ketchup down its front. A little bit of ketchup is also in the girl's hair.

"Uh, sorta," I say, and I demonstrate the coaster flip one more time.

"Coooooooooool." The girl tries to snatch a coaster of her own, but she's barely tall enough to reach the top of the bar, let alone flip the coaster and catch it in midair.

"Here." I bring one down to her and toss it straight up into the air like a Frisbee and catch it again. It's not even a trick, but she seems enthralled. She grabs the coaster with both of her tiny hands and waddles off to show someone else the miracle that is gravity.

Since the bar-trick thing didn't attract anyone over the age of eight, I decide to take a more aggressive approach with Ryan Gosling Bartender. He's slouched against the fake wooden wall behind the bar, still playing with his phone.

"Hey," I say. He looks up. "How's it going?"

He shrugs. "Not too bad, I guess. You?"

I look down at the cocktail napkin. "I guess I'm doing . . . all *Wright-Holmes*."

He doesn't laugh at my terrible dad joke, and I can feel my neck getting hot. "WHISKEY, STRAIGHT UP," I say loudly.

The bartender slides his phone into his pocket and turns to look at me, one eyebrow cocked. *Oh god, why did I say that? What does "straight up" even mean? He's going to ask for an ID and call the police, and I'm going to get kicked out of my own father's wedding. There's no way my mom is going to let me go to Europe alone if she has to bail me out of jail for underage drinking. What was I thinking? I don't even LIKE whiskey. I'm pretty sure it tastes like someone burned down a log cabin using chemicals of questionable legality.*

Before the bartender even has time to react, I duck below the line of the bar so quickly that there should be a cartoon *whoosh!* sound effect. As I contemplate whether to continue crawling along the length of the bar or make a break for it toward the bathroom, I hear a voice crack through the murmur and music of the party.

"Nora!"

Instinctually, I freeze. Still, somewhere deep inside my animal brain, I associate that voice with not knowing Euler's theorem. Hearing Ms. Wright call out my name autocompletes in my head to "Have you got the homework for today?"

She's wearing a long-sleeved lace dress that would probably be pretty if it weren't on the math teacher marrying my dad. She's also still wearing her red, thick-framed glasses. You'd think a person would want to take those off for her own wedding, but I guess she's a fan of the librarian-with-eleven-cats look. I wouldn't have gone with mint green and peach as a color scheme for a wedding either, but to each her own, I guess.

"Nora! You look . . ." Ms. Wright—*Tina*—pauses, as if she's deciding whether or not to acknowledge the fact that I'm currently crouching on the sticky floor of a hotel ballroom.

"Dropped something," I say, quickly standing up. "It's great to see you. Thank you so much for having me."

She looks confused. My dad comes up behind her, wrapping his arm around her waist. It took about a year of seeing them together before I could witness something like this without dry-heaving, but now I've reached the point of almost being able to contain a grimace.

"Sweetheart. You look fantastic."

That's the thing about dads: They never *actually* know when you look fantastic. He has no idea that this dress is almost six years old or that I spent a grand total of thirty-seven seconds on my makeup because I was running very, very late to a ceremony in which I had the all-important job of reading a poem (*"I carry your heart with me. I carry it in my heart"*). But I smile and give my dad a hug, careful not to rip the taffeta of my dress as I raise my arm. And, in the spirit of gracious benevolence, I give a hug to my new stepmom, Tina, even though she's wearing red-framed glasses to her own wedding and chose a mint-green-and-peach color scheme.

Tina looks over at my dad, then back at me. "Nora, we are just so happy you're here and a member of our family. And we just want to let you know that of course you're welcome in Arizona any time."

Dad smiles and pats me on the shoulder. "It's our home. I mean, *your* home too, really. Tell Alice—I mean, tell your mother—that we say you're welcome any time."

I don't respond. Tina looks at the floor. The sweat gathering in my armpits decides to amp up production. My dad clears his throat and continues, "Your mother couldn't make it tonight, huh?"

"No," I say, not making eye contact. "Stomach thing."

We all know I'm lying.

"She's—everything's good otherwise?" Dad asks the floor.

"Yeah," I say.

I notice the way Tina and my dad both fidget with their rings the moment Alice comes up.

Do I tell them that I still hear Mom crying in the bathroom sometimes? Or that she demands to know the first and last name of every single person I'll be hanging out with every time I want to go out with a group of friends that includes one or more guys, even though I'm about to be a senior in high school? Or that every morning she presents me with a new article she printed about how many artists don't make a living wage and how I need to fall back on "practical skills, like engineering, or math, or science, Nora, something you can actually use to get a *job*. I know my father was successful as an artist, but you need to remember in addition to being extremely lucky, he didn't sell his first painting until he was forty-five years old. Are you really willing to wait that long, Nora?"

"She's great," I say. "We're both great."

My dad takes a step closer and claps a hand on my shoulder. "Nora is going to be traveling to Europe to work on her art this summer," he tells Tina, and I wonder why she doesn't already know. "Which cities are you traveling to again?"

"Paris, Brussels, and then three weeks at the Donegal Colony for Young Artists, and then Florence, and then London, and then home," I recite.

"An artists' colony!" Tina practically yelps. "That's a big deal, Nora!"

I start liking her a little more.

Dad gives me a squeeze. "You have more talent in your little finger than I have in my entire body. Must have gotten it all from the Robert Parker genes."

Just then, a woman in a dress like a big-top tent begins to tear up at Tina's elbow, and the two of them screech and hug and Dad gives me a look that seems to say, *Women, right?* We share a smile, and we don't talk anymore about Mom, because he and I both realize he should be worrying about cutting the cake, and giving a speech, and moving from Chicago to Arizona.

He doesn't need to worry anymore about the sad, bitter divorced woman who just became exclusively my problem.

3

"OKAY, I'M JUST telling you, no one in Europe wears jeans."

"What?"

Lena holds up the pair of boyfriend jeans I spent a full five seconds folding and throws them across the room. "My sister studied abroad in Barcelona, and that's what she said."

I twirl the green streak around my finger and stare for a few seconds at the already overstuffed carry-on sitting on my carpet. "Okay, but then what do they wear?"

"I don't know," Lena says. "Leggings? Skirts? Probably skirts. Everyone is way fancier over there. If you're not, like, in heels and a sweater or something, they'll know you're a tourist. Or a scarf! People wear scarves in Europe!"

"Well, I don't have a scarf. What about these?" I hold up my New Balance sneakers. "Should I just not bring gym shoes?" I pass the shoes to Lena. She smells them for absolutely no conceivable reason.

"Do you have, like, nicer gym shoes?"

My knees creak and pop as I stand up from sitting down for so long, trying to fit half a closet into a suitcase twenty inches long ("European airlines have different carry-on restrictions," Lena told me knowingly).

"How about these?" I extract a pair of Vans from the floor of my closet. They're still scribbled with pop-punk lyrics I wrote in Sharpie back when everyone in middle school was struck with the collective delusion that that was cool. I wind up like a softball pitcher and throw one as hard as I can at Lena.

"Ow!"

"Oh, shut up, you know that didn't actually hurt."

Lena rubs an invisible lump on her arm. "It hurt a *little*." She forgets the pain as soon as she notices the writing on the white rubber sole. "Oh my god, 'You call me up again just to break me like a promise'? What is this, The Script?"

I grab the shoe back and attempt to fit both sneakers along the side of the bag. I manage to get them in, only slightly displacing my raincoat. "You know full well it's Taylor Swift." I sing, a little louder than I need to, with mock-angst, over-exaggerated diction: "*You call me up again just to break me like a promise. So something something in the name of being honest.*"

"'Casually cruel,'" Lena supplies.

"Ha! I knew you knew it! Don't pretend you didn't try to cut your own bangs when you saw Taylor had them."

Lena slides onto her stomach. "Oh my god, I think Nick cut his own hair last year, because he had the worst haircut in the world. Hold on, I'll find a picture." She's already extracted her phone from her back pocket before I can say a word. She swipes past a few old photos from Nick's Facebook. I've seen them all a dozen times—poorly focused shots of Nick in striped Hollister polos with the promised terrible haircut uneven on his forehead, not quite covering the craters of early teenage acne on his face.

Just as I reach to grab the phone to get a better view, Lena pulls away. "Oh my god, I'm really sorry."

"It's fine," I say, and I almost mean it.

"No, you asked me not to talk about him. I'm sorry."

"It's been . . ." I think for a moment. "Months."

Here's where, in my imagination, Lena turns to me and says something like, "No, I can tell that it still bothers you, and of course it would. Even though you didn't *date* Nick that doesn't mean you didn't have feelings for him, and as your best friend I should respect that." Or, ideally, even better: "Oh my god, I forgot to mention, you were so right about Nick. He is a colossal douchenozzle of a human being, a parasitic emotional vampire who makes girls think he cares about them and then moves on when he gets attention from someone else. How did I not see it before? Every girl at NSHS knows now, and no one is going to date him ever again."

Instead, she rolls over once, checking Twitter on her phone. "Honestly, I totally see exactly what you said about him. Sometimes I ask myself why I still want to date him at all when he can be such an asshole. Like, flirting with other girls in front of me? Sorry, I mean, obviously you know better than anyone."

I want to shout at her, "If you can see it, then why do you want to date him at all?" But I don't. I get off the bed and sift through my makeup, trying to figure out what will fit in a Ziploc baggie. It's my own stupid fault for not saying anything when she asked whether it would be weird if she and Nick hung out together, just once.

"Oh my god, of course not!" I said, doing my best impression of the *super chill girl who never had feelings for Nick at all because the two of you were never actually dating.*

It's too late for that. Now I just need to empty my brain completely of Nick and refill it with anxiety about the trip.

"Okay," I say. "So . . . one pair of jeans—" Lena raises an eyebrow. "*Dark wash jeans.* One pair of leggings. Two T-shirts, one going-out top. And all the underwear I can fit."

"So how are you going to get the, um, projects back to your grandpa? Like, are you going to keep them in your suitcase? Or . . . ?"

Shit. I didn't think this through. "Do you think I should bring stamps? Wait, it's different in Europe. Fuck, I didn't think of that."

One of the caveats of my free trip to Europe is that, in addition to visiting the best museums in each city, I have to complete assignments of Grandpa's choice and send the resulting pieces back to him. The sealed manila envelopes are still on my desk, each labeled in Grandpa's all-caps handwriting: PARIS,

GHENT, FLORENCE, LONDON. I'm under strict instruction not to open each one until I get to the corresponding city.

Lena spreads out the envelopes like a card shark and fans herself. "Why don't you ask your mom how he wants you to send them? Or, like, ask her if they have FedEx in Belgium." She uses the envelopes to make it rain like she's in a rap music video.

"Ha." I pick the folders up and file them neatly in the front compartment of my backpack. "We haven't even spoken in days. It's like a stranger rented a room in our house on Airbnb."

"Practice for college, I guess?" Lena says.

"Did you know dorms at RISD are coed? When do you think I should let that tidbit slide into a conversation with my mom about my future?"

"How's your application going, by the way?" Lena asks. She, of course, being the perfect paradox of a stoner overachiever that she is, has already finished writing personal essays for her first *fifteen* choices. We've been planning for her to go to Brown and for me to go to RISD since eighth grade.

"It'll be going much better," I take on an exaggerated French accent, "wheen I zee all oof zee fine art zhat Yuuurupe haz to offer." I take a drag on an invisible cigarette and twirl a curlicue mustache.

"What's the place you're going to called again?"

"Donegal Colony for Young Artists. DCYA. Do I need to make another Post-It note to stick to the back of your phone so you remember?" Maybe it's all the pot, but Lena has a terrible memory.

She doesn't answer. Instead, she slides across my bed like it's the hood of a cop car in an action movie. "IT'S FUN TO STAY AT THE D-C-Y-A! It's fun to stay at the D-C-Y-A." She struggles to figure out arm positions that create a convincing *D*. I refuse to engage. I'm back to packing.

"Are you going to update your Tumblr while you're gone?" Lena is the first, and possibly only, fangirl for Ophelia in Paradise, the Tumblr where I upload all the cartoons I draw—some of the commissions and some that I've just doodled for myself. My own doodles are mostly modern-day versions of characters from books I read. A drawing of Katniss Everdeen representing Team USA in archery at the Olympics got, like, eight hundred thousand reblogs.

"I don't think so," I say. "I mean, I could, but I figure I'll be busy with my grandpa's assignments and with the DCYA stuff."

"Hey," Lena says. "You're not going to have to take a train to the airport, are you?"

I had told Lena how terrible it was getting to my dad's wedding, going downtown on the Metro in my tight dress and heels. My mom never once offered to drive me. I hadn't even realized she had declined on the RSVP until the night before.

I pull my favorite set of pencils from the Tupperware under my desk and put it in my backpack, along with the new spiral of drawing paper I bought this morning.

"I don't *think* so. I mean, my mom's at least going to want to say good-bye to her only daughter, right?" When I came home from the wedding, she was already in her bedroom, maybe asleep, and so I didn't say good night.

It suddenly dawns on me that it's very possible my mom isn't driving me to the airport after all. Maybe in our sullen obstinacy over the past few days, we cemented a tacit pact that even though I'm technically allowed to go Europe on her father's dime, Alice Parker will do absolutely nothing to encourage my behavior. "I need to Google train schedules. Does the train even run that early?"

"What time do you need to leave?"

Before I can answer, my door swings open, revealing my mother: five foot three inches tall, newly minted paralegal, and parental nightmare.

"Did you get home late last night?" she asks, not even bothering to look at Lena, let alone say hi. I give Lena an apologetic look, hoping she'll forgive me for my mom being so rude. Usually she loves Lena, offering her an endless array of snacks that she's never offered me and begging for stories about Lena's little twin brothers.

"Yeah," I say. "Around two, I think? I took an Uber from the train station."

"Fifteen dollars or so?" She pulls an androgynous leather wallet out of her purse and extracts two bills, which I stand to take.

"Thanks."

I wait a minute to see whether she's going to ask about the wedding. She clears her throat and smooths out the hem of her skirt.

"Your father looked well?" she finally says.

Lena looks at me. "Yeah," I say. "He looked good." How am I supposed to respond? He did look well. Happier than I've ever seen him, if I'm being completely honest. "His hair got longer."

My mother opens her mouth slightly and then closes it again without saying anything.

In my head, I play out a scene where I smile and tell her how terrible the halibut was. We'd laugh about how much we hate Arizona and how sad it is that Dad had to go and marry someone who would drag him off to the land of strip malls to be closer to her family. I could say something about how sad I feel about it too, about the hole he's leaving, like a dry socket where a tooth was removed.

But then I see the way my mom eyes the paint supplies I already packed, and the words dissolve like a Listerine strip on my tongue.

"Wouldn't you rather use that room in your suitcase for a more practical pair of shoes." She says it as a statement, not a question.

"Uh, no. I need the art supplies to complete the assignments Grandpa's having me do in each stop."

Her frown tightens.

Lena coughs, and my mom and I both look at her. Alice directs her attention back to me with a single sharp turn of her head. "So your flight is at eleven A.M. We'll leave the house at eight forty-five," she says. And then she turns to walk down the hall to her bedroom.

"See you in the car," I call after her. She's already gone.

Lena and I are quiet for a few minutes as I fold clothes as tightly as I can so that they'll fit into the unfathomably tiny carry-on that I'll be living out of. Suddenly, Lena gets off my bed and begins examining the paintings I've hung above my desk. They're portraits, of us mostly, created using only primary colors, with bold lines like a comic book. Even when I'm not drawing cartoons for Tumblr, that's the style I always seem to fall back on. "God, I love these," Lena says.

"Oh, gross, no." I stand, cracking the knuckles of both of my hands out of habit, and walk over to run my finger along the edge of one of the canvases. At the time I painted them, I thought they were so good, like, *call the MoMA now and set up a debut for a brilliant young talent!* But now, just six months later, I only see flat, sloppy brushstrokes, like a middle-schooler's paint-by-numbers.

"What if—" I pause, take a breath, and start again. "What if I'm the worst one at the colony? What if they kick me out after the first workshop?"

"Then fuck 'em," Lena says.

"Thank you," I say. "Very comforting."

Lena realizes she made a mistake; her face falls, and she takes half a step backward. "Hey," she says, sitting on my bed and patting for me to sit next to her. I do. "You're great, honestly. You're going to do amazing stuff. You'll probably be the best artist there by a long shot. And then you're going to meet some hot Scottish boy and fall madly in love and go off and be an art couple like Frida Kahlo and Geraldo Rivera."

For the first time all day, I actually feel my facial muscles unclench, and I smile. "*Geraldo* Rivera?"

"Yeah," Lena says, a grin making its way across her face. "What? Geraldo Rivera."

* * *

For the next twelve hours, I tell myself I don't need to worry about whether my art will be good enough, or how I'll find a post office to send my paintings to Grandpa, or whether I'll have to give my mom a kiss and pretend that I'll miss her when she drops me off at the airport. All I think about is calculating exactly how good the odds are that I'll meet a Scottish artist named Geraldo Rivera while I'm in Ireland.

4

I CALCULATE THE risk-to-reward ratio of changing the radio in my mom's car from NPR to a pop station. Honestly, I kind of want to do it just to get under her skin. There's something too curated, too oddly staged, about the two of us riding, backs straight, mouths closed, on the still-empty roads of the early morning while some woman half-whispers news about Bangladesh.

The impulse strikes me. I pull my hand from paralyzing stillness and twist the radio knob until I hear a heavy synth beat. I would have turned the volume up as well, just to really make a scene of it, but it's too early in the morning even for me to want to deal with throbbing eardrums.

THIS TIME, BABY

I'LL BE
BULLETPROOF

"Excuse me," Mom says, but she doesn't bring her hands from the wheel to change the radio back.

THIS TIME, BABY
I'LL BE-E-EEE
BULLETPROOF

"Sorry," I say, but I don't change it back either.

We listen to the overproduced techno until the song ends and the station moves on to a commercial for a carpet-cleaning service. My mom turns the radio off with a quick, certain tap of her manicured fingers.

We allowed ourselves a full hour to get to O'Hare Airport from Evanston this morning, but with the clear roads, we're almost there in a third of that time. I watch my mom, her elbows still, her eyes fixed on the bumper of the Volvo ahead of us, her mouth slightly twitching as if silently mouthing the words to a song she was embarrassed to like.

Fuck it. I pull my sketchpad out of the backpack between my knees.

"Do you *think*—" my mom begins sharply before stopping to take a deep breath. I begin doodling lyrics from songs stuck in my head, stretching out lines until they fill a whole page.

THIS TIME, BABY, I'LL BE BULLETPROOF.

My mother's eyes jerk from the road to my sketchpad and back. "Very antisocial behavior, Nora," she says.

"Oh, I'm sorry for ignoring the sparkling conversation of this car ride."

Mom rolls to a stop at a red light and turns so that her shoulders are square to me. "You really think—I mean, this focus on *art* . . ."

"This 'focus on art' is basically my life," I interrupt. "So . . . thanks."

She takes a deep breath through her nose. "I apologize. But spending a whole summer at this . . . this camp. Don't you think you could be more *productive* spending time with people with varied, well-rounded interests? Or finishing your real college applications?"

I don't make eye contact when I answer. "Honestly, the reason I'm so excited for Ireland is because, for the first time in my life, I'll be completely surrounded by people who truly understand what art means to me. How much I care about it."

"I understand it's a fulfilling hobby, but you're usually so responsible, and in terms of making a good choice for your college major and career—"

"If I'm usually so responsible, then you should trust me to make my own decision," I say. "Because I'm heading into adulthood. And at some point, adults get to make decisions about what they want to do with their lives."

"But you're not an adult yet, Nora," she says. "I am. And I care about your *future*."

"Well, my future will be spent in Europe, and then at college, and then away from Evanston for the rest of my life," I respond, before turning my full attention back to my sketchpad.

Mom and I don't speak for the rest of the car ride. In the stony, heavy silence, neither of us dares to turn on the radio. Our car crawls through the winding overpasses, following signs with arrows above the words INTERNATIONAL DEPARTURES.

A traffic attendant motions for us to pull forward into an empty strip by the front of a glass building, and before the car even stops I pull my backpack onto my lap and sling an arm through the shoulder strap.

"Don't forget your carry-on, in the trunk," my mother says.

"I won't."

I wait outside the car, backpack on, handle raised on the carry-on. My mother has decided to get out of the car and stand on the driver's side.

"Well," I say. "Thanks for the ride."

"Text me when you land in Paris."

I know I should say, "I love you," the same way how, when you're lying in bed at eight on a Monday morning, you know you should actually get up and brush your teeth. You can visualize yourself doing it, walk yourself through every step in your head, but when you come back to reality, you're still there, in bed, teeth unbrushed, not actually doing what you told yourself to do.

"Thanks for the ride," I say again. And I turn, walking toward the automatic doors that just pulled open with an antiseptic whoosh.

"*WAIT!*"

At first I don't realize that the voice is directed at me. I definitely don't realize it belongs to my mother. My first thought? *How embarrassing for whoever is getting in a fight at the airport.* My second thought (when I realize that the voice came from the row of cars in Departures) is that someone is getting in a fight with the traffic attendant in charge of parking. Also embarrassing.

But then I see Alice Parker speed-walking through the doors—our car blinking its hazard lights behind her—and my stomach pulls up into my throat. I pat my pockets and backpack to see if I forgot my passport. *Nope.* I just stare at her face and wonder what I could have possibly done wrong already, fourteen seconds into my trip.

"I'm coming with you," she says, panting.

"Like, through security?"

"No." She straightens. "This trip. Europe. The first leg, at least—until you get to Ireland. What's first? Paris and Belgium?" Already her eyes are scanning the American Airlines desks, looking for an available agent who can help her buy a ticket.

"What? You're . . . I mean, you're not packed," I say, my tongue feeling thicker in my mouth than usual.

She sighs and looks in my eyes for the first time all day. "You're leaving. But . . ." As she searches for the right phrase, a couple in matching tracksuits and sporting deep purple under-eye circles shoves their way through us with rolling suitcases. My mom tries again. "You're pulling. We're pulling apart, and it isn't fair. You're leaving for college so soon, and you're so busy with your friends, and I'm so busy with work. I just realized that I don't know you at all. Like the music on the radio—I didn't even know you listened to that sort of music."

"I don't!" I say. "I didn't even know that song. Honestly. It was just what was on the radio!"

"I don't *know* you, Nora," she continues, acting like she hasn't even heard me. "And I'm not going to waste this opportunity to get to know you."

"What about work? How can you just leave for, like, a month?"

Her face darkens for a moment, but then immediately recovers. "I can take of it."

"I wanted to do this on my own," I say. I don't know why my throat is tightening like I'm about to cry.

"But you don't have to!" my mother says, eyes bright, lips peeled apart.

My visions of wandering alone and carefree through the streets of Paris and London suddenly dissolve. Where I had been drinking espresso and leisurely eating a chocolate croissant while reading a book in French (in my fantasy, I speak French), I now see myself plodding alongside Alice Parker, both of us in jeans and terrible sneakers, trying to make it to some tour I don't care about.

She places her hands on my shoulders with a little too much force.

"I am so excited," she says, still scanning behind me for someone to help her buy a ticket to ruin my summer.

"Yeah," I reply. But I can't force myself to say, "Me too."

5

IT'S A RUSH of phone calls in the car ride home, my mom's voice oscillating wildly between confrontational and saccharine as she talks to the airline employees on the other end of the line. I think I fall asleep for most of the ride, hoodie pulled over my head, cheek against the window. If someone were filming this in black and white, it would be a very dramatic shot in a music video. Adele's voice should be warbling over this scene.

I resist the urge to sigh loudly when I drop my suitcase in the hallway. My mother doesn't notice that her only daughter is upset; she heads straight to the breakfast-nook-turned-office and begins typing furiously at her keyboard, as if the harder she presses, the faster her dinosaur of a PC will respond.

"Would you rather stay at the Maison Robespierre or at the place I found off the Rue De La Grande?" my mom asks without looking up from her computer.

"I don't care," I say. I spent hours over the past few weeks combing through backpacker message boards to find a hostel with high recommendations for "MEETING NEW PEOPLE!" (and with free WiFi), but that was all for when this trip was mine.

"Of course you care," she replies. "Which do you prefer?"

But the truth of the matter is, I really don't, because my choice has already been taken away. All the preparation, all the excitement, all the daydreams about traveling on my own—they're escaping me, leaving me a hollow shell nodding at every meaningless hotel or restaurant name Alice throws at me. I had already fully imagined the Facebook album I'd be uploading throughout the trip: images of me sipping coffee in Paris, meeting a roving gang of artists, kissing a stranger on the cheek while we both laugh. *Wow*, everyone back home would say. *That Nora sure is an adventurous and independent free spirit. I guess we all underestimated her.*

Now, though, I'll be posting pictures from a family vacation. No, not even a family vacation. The only thing lamer: a mother-daughter bonding trip. And with my mother, who still thinks a fanny pack is an acceptable article of clothing to wear unironically or outside of a music festival.

In the span of a couple of hours, I've gone from European adventuress to prisoner. What does it matter which hotel room is going to be my cell?

"I already have a hostel reservation," I say.

"Don't be silly, we're not staying at a *youth* hostel." My mom practically spits the words at me. "You can stay with me at the hotel!" She sips the coffee that she had left on the counter to drive me to the airport and winces slightly at how bitter it is cold. "Wouldn't you so much rather have clean sheets? Maid service?"

"Well, you know, you stay in a big room in a hostel, you get to make friends," I say to my feet. She doesn't hear me.

"We'll have our own big, beautiful room!" Her grin is sickeningly proud.

The worst part about all of this is the generosity that oozes out with every word my mother says, as if I'm supposed to be grateful to stay at some random hotel instead of a hostel where I might meet some cute British boy with an accent and messy hair who would make me forget that Nick ever existed. Now, even if I do meet him, there's going to be nowhere for us to hang out.

ME: I forgot to mention that I'm a huge dork. Come back and meet my mom!

HIM: Actually I just realized that I am not attracted to you at all in any way. Lovely to meet you, I'm going to go back to the hostel with a seven-foot-tall blonde Dutch girl who is old enough to travel by herself.

I sit on the couch and put my feet up on my still-zipped suitcase. "What about your *job*?"

My mom takes a large gulp of coffee, forgetting that it's cold and a silvery film is already forming on its surface. She grimaces. "I told you. It's fine. I took care of it." When I don't respond, she goes on. "I can work remotely, Nora. This isn't the third world. They'll have WiFi. I handled it."

I guess I missed that phone call in the unending flurry of tasks my mother seemed to complete without a second thought. I begin to wonder if my mother had planned this all along. Had she watched me for weeks as I booked hostels and bought guidebooks, waiting for the best time to weasel her way into my trip? Prepared to pounce when I was too tired and over-whelmed to come up with a good reason why she shouldn't join me?

My paranoia is interrupted by a text from Lena: *I know you're on a plane right now, but have THE BEST time in Paris and send me 17 postcards and a croissant. Also you're so brave.* Usually when I get a text message, I reply immediately out of habit. But now, looking at her message, I get a sensation in my stomach akin to a fifty-pound rock dropping into a shallow pond. There's no emoji for "Looks like I'm going to have a cur-few when I'm traveling throughout Europe after all! Good-bye, discotheques; hello, matinees of *Cats* in the West End!"

And so I don't respond, and to the percussive backbeat of my mother pecking at her keyboard, I start scrolling through Instagram. My finger lingers on a picture of Lena kissing Nick's cheek at a soccer game, which makes me feel only slightly less nauseated than the prospect of spending weeks in Europe with Alice Parker. Is it too much to ask that after you break up with someone, they should be forced to move to Canada and never interact with anyone you know ever again? *You're not in love with him*, I tell myself in my most grown-up voice. *That way your stomach clenches when you think of him isn't love. It's jealousy, infatuation, regret, embarrassment, lust—anything but love. Mind over matter! Excelsior!*

I scroll past, proud of myself, through the pictures of skeletal fashion bloggers posing with bug-eyed sunglasses and mucus-green juices. They've all mastered the same look: marble countertop with a magazine, headphones, coffee, and a designer lipstick accidentally-on-purpose strewn to look artistically askew.

I close Instagram, and, for the millionth time, I open the DCYA website on my laptop and am greeted by photos of the idyllic Irish countryside and students painting on canvases and posing together by a lighthouse. A SUMMER OF ARTISTIC GROWTH AND FRIENDSHIP reads a banner at the top of the page.

I'm temporarily comforted by the fact that I'll eventually be one of the students in those pictures, smiling a vague stock-photo-model smile and posing by an Irish lighthouse with new friends. And none of those friends will be dating a boy I used to be in love with.

Within forty minutes, my mother finishes packing her suitcase and, with a few claps, shepherds me into the car to drive back to O'Hare, this time by the light of full morning.

After my mother finishes a final, curt phone call to some poor woman at United ("Thank you, *Deborah*. Have a lovely day."), we're left to sit in silence.

"Is your suitcase under twenty inches?" I ask. I know the answer, but I'm picking a fight. I'm entitled, okay? My mom—who doesn't know the first thing about art, I should say, who wouldn't know her Monet from her Michelangelo—made the unilateral decision to completely upend my trip. I'm allowed to rub in the fact that I was the only one who prepared.

She doesn't reply.

"Twenty inches," I repeat. "Your suitcase?"

"What?" she says, not looking away from the road. "No, it's my tan suitcase. Twenty-three inches."

"UGH. European airlines are *different*, Mom! They charge, like, more than the actual flight for checking luggage, and their overhead compartments are smaller! Rick Steves *specified* that if you're traveling throughout Europe, you should only have a carry-on. That's what he does."

"Who is Rick Steve?" my mother asks, completely missing the point.

"*Steves.* And he's, like, the European travel-guru guy. You're going to have to check your bag if it's bigger that twenty inches."

"Well, if I have to, I'll check the bag," she says in a reserved voice.

My voice comes out louder than I intended. "And that leaves me where? Waiting by the luggage carousel for you when I could be out, I don't know, meeting new people? Exploring a new city like I was *supposed* to be doing?"

My mom turns to me with that Mom look and a pause that usually means I'm about to have car privileges revoked, but then her face softens. It's the face she makes when she sees an acquaintance at the grocery store who doesn't know that she and Dad are divorced. *Hide your left hand.* "Yes, we're doing wonderfully, thank you for asking."

"I know a trip with your mom may not sound like fun on paper, but I'm so excited to spend some time with you, Nora!"

I tighten my lips into something that might be a smile but is probably closer to a dog with peanut butter on the roof of his mouth.

Mom senses my moment of weakness and moves in for the kill. "You're going to miss me when you're away next year."

Whatever response I had dissolves like a lump of sugar in my throat, and I silently vow to try to be a good sport to my mom for as long as I can. I don't even draw in the car on the way back to the airport. My mom asks me to pick the radio station. Clearly she's trying her best too.

Because of the last-minute ticket purchasing, both my mom and I have tickets in middle seats. While we wait at Gate 2B, I scan through the other passengers en route to Paris and make a mental roster of who might be flanking me on the eight-hour flight to come.

Option 1: *A couple, both with flaxen-blond hair and stained sweatpants, fishing in the bottom of their McDonalds bags. I silently pray I won't be surrounded by the smell of McSweat for the entire trip.*

Option 2: *An impossibly cool-looking girl with inky black bangs who bobs her head along to whatever beat is pulsing through her massive headphones while reading a copy of* Mein Kampf. *This girl is either far cooler than anyone*

I have ever seen in Evanston, Illinois, or she's a neo-Nazi.
Fifty-fifty odds.

Option 3: *A model-handsome man with red hair and a*
ginger beard, someone who should probably be cast on a
premium-cable television show about nineteenth-century
Scotland if he hasn't been already. A venous arm is slung
around his girlfriend, a woman with a chubby round face
and long hair down to her butt. Her hand is on his knee. I
imagine the PDA I'd be enduring with those two on either
side of me. Is it possible for STIs to go airborne?

I'm feeling fairly hopeless, when suddenly I see a boy—a
man, really—with an undercut and a full tattoo sleeve. He's
reading Joan Didion and has a guitar case between his feet.
I think one of his tattoos might be a dwarf from *Lord of the*
Rings.

Still looking at him, I pull out my sketchbook, hoping
he'll notice that I'm also an artist. I flip to the next empty
page and draw a punk rock Elizabeth Bennett from *Pride and*
Prejudice, looking up at the boy—*man*—after every pencil
stroke. He doesn't look at me. I concentrate on my face, hoping to look introspective and focused on my pencil movements. I bite my lip. If he looks over right now, he'll see a sexy,
determined artist too focused on her casually amazing sketch
to even look up.

Please let him be seated next to me. Please let him ask to see
my sketchbook and think my designs are perfect for his album

cover, and please let him secretly be an about-to-become-famous musician. Please let us wander the streets of Paris together, working on our art. "Wow," he'll say quietly, as we sit at a café and he sips espresso while watching me sketch, "you're . . . that's amazing." But he'll actually say it in French, because he's fluent in French.

And when we go to the Grammys together, the paparazzi will whisper, "That girl he's with, she's the one who did the iconic design on the album cover. Can you believe they met on a plane to Paris?"

Once I'm boarded with my book on my lap and my economical (twenty-inch!) carry-on appropriately stowed in the overhead compartment, I watch the rest of the passengers trudge through the aisles with the dead, listless gaits of zombies in a Romero movie. My mother has already settled herself two rows ahead of me, her head cradled by a blue nylon neck pillow. A dour businessman with a laptop that looks like it's from 1987 has claimed the aisle seat of my row, but the window remains mercifully free. I breathe a sigh of relief when the four girls in Ugg boots slide into the row ahead of me, and again when I spot the McDonald's couple disappear into their seats at the front of the plane. As the line of passengers thins, I see the boy—my future fiancé and artistic partner—making his way toward my row. *Maybe if I stare hard enough, he'll feel my gaze and make eye contact.*

Five rows to go.

He's definitely coming to sit here.

Four rows.

This is the first time one of my imaginary scenarios has actually panned out.

Three rows.

Okay, time to look back at my book. I can't be staring at him when he gets here.

I open the novel in my lap and force myself to concentrate on the words as my skin prickles and I wait to hear his voice: "Excuse me, that's my seat in the window there."

I read a sentence in my book, then the same sentence again, and then a third time. Thirty seconds pass, and I realize it's been too long. Just as I'm deciding whether or not to look up, a woman's voice breaks the silence.

"Just there," she says.

The businessman and I rise to let her in, and while I'm in the aisle, I notice that the guy with the guitar case and cool tattoos and handsome eyes has taken a seat right next to my mother.

Of course.

I spend the rest of the flight in and out of an uncomfortable sleep. At one point, I think my mom comes by to check on me, but I force myself to keep my eyes shut. I read half a chapter of *Invisible Man*, our summer reading assignment for AP English lit, that I barely remember, except that at one point I made a mental note to draw one of the scenes for Ophelia in Paradise, but now I have no idea which.

By the time the captain declares (in an impossible-to-place accent) that flight attendants should prepare for landing, I have no idea whether we've been on the plane for ten minutes or ten hours. The entire metal tube with its flickering dim lights and the omniscient headphone buzz has become a world unto itself.

The cabin lights ding to life, and the businessman lifts his head from an uncomfortable-looking angle, glaring at me as if his neck problems tomorrow will be my fault.

My mother waits for me just outside the plane doors, looking far less sleepy than I'm sure I do. She asks how my flight was, and I say it was fine. I ask how her flight was, and she says fine. Sparkling conversation, really.

"Sit next to anyone interesting?" I ask. Maybe she and the boy bonded, and we're all going to meet up in Paris.

"I didn't notice," she replies.

"Can I get a coffee or muffin or something?" I say, realizing exactly how hungry I am for the first time now that I'm eyeing an airport Starbucks.

"We're in an *airport*," she says without even looking at me, and she begins striding away, her shoes clicking on the linoleum floor. It's the exact walk I can imagine her using to intimidate clients in her office. "Besides," she adds, "you shouldn't be getting *Starbucks* in Paris. We'll be at our hotel soon. I looked up the address, and there are a dozen *patisseries* on the same block."

She pronounces *patisseries* like a pretentious college junior who just got back from six months studying abroad in France.

"But I'm hungry now." If I were traveling alone, I'd be able to eat what I want, when I want, and not have to deal with any snobbery about an airport muffin.

My mom gives an exaggerated sigh and fishes in her pocket, pulling out an open bag of raw almonds. "Here," she says. "This is why you should plan ahead for this sort of thing."

Hungry as I am, I can't think of anything less appetizing than my mom's pocket almonds. "Thanks," I mumble and transfer the bag into my own pocket.

Then, because my mother hadn't realized how much easier it is just to bring a carry-on to Europe instead of checking a bag, the two of us drudge side by side toward baggage claim like zombie versions of the girls from *Madeline*. Yet another delay before I can get real food.

"Why don't you get us a taxi?" My mom pulls her suitcase from the luggage carousel. "I need to make some calls."

"For work?"

"No, not for work," she snaps. "I just need to take care of a few more reservations for the trip."

I sense something in her, something evasive and sharp like a splinter buried deep under skin.

"You don't need to call anyone at work?" I ask, pressing.

"No," she says, checking her nail beds to make sure they're as pristine as ever. "I do not, thank you."

So my mother just made the impromptu decision to take a weeks-long trip with me overseas, and now she has no more calls to make for work or frantic e-mails to return? An itching realization creeps into my head. *She probably told them about this trip a month ago. What if she's been planning to come the whole time?*

That's what my brain keeps whispering to me on the silent

cab ride through the dark Paris streets, still buzzing with life even at midnight. My mom had given directions in slow, deliberate French, well enough that the cab driver understood her.

By the time we finally arrive, the lobby is empty aside from a single sleepy teenage concierge who hands us a large brass key after plucking my mom's credit card out of her hands. There's no restaurant in the hotel. I pull an almond from my pocket and eat it miserably. It tastes like sawdust and sadness.

Tomorrow I will look at the city, at the art, at this entirely new landmass that I had to fly across an ocean to see. Tomorrow I'll visit places I've only seen pictures of and eat pastries that look like spun silk. Tomorrow my eyes will be less puffy and watery and my skin will be less dry.

But tonight I'll dig through my clothes to find a toothbrush and drag myself into a twin bed with a flat, heavy blanket, and I'll fall asleep so that this day can finally be over.

6

THE ROOM THAT looked musty and mothballed in the glare of an outside streetlamp and the dreary haze of my exhaustion takes on new life in the light of the morning. The wallpaper is a soft yellow fabric that matches an upholstered chair in the corner and the pillows I swept off the bed in a bleary-eyed huff last night. Now, the entire hotel room looks like a Cézanne painting, wide brushstroke swatches the color of sunrise.

My mom is already awake, tightening the laces on her gym shoes.

"I'm sorry about yesterday," she says as I emerge from the bathroom post-shower (and post-exploratory use of the squat porcelain bidet).

"'S okay," I say. I wonder what I should be wearing today. Lena had said something about skirts. Did I bring a scarf? I wish I remembered to bring a scarf.

My mom clears her throat. "I'd love to show you the Paris I remember. I studied abroad here! You know that, right?" It sounds like she's reciting a speech she rehearsed.

I eye my sketchpad and watercolors. "I had sort of planned to go the Delacroix museum today—"

"We can do that too! Afterward. Let's do breakfast, a few shops. I have to take you to the bakery I went to every day when I was in college. And then the Delacroix museum?"

The prospect of breakfast and a bakery is pretty persuasive. And, as long as we go to the Musée Delacroix afterward, I figure I can allow myself to be seduced by a flaky croissant and a tour guide who knows Paris better than I do, even if she hasn't been back in twenty-five years. To be honest, there are not many things I would not be agreeable to if a croissant is offered first. "It sounds like a plan."

I'm significantly happier than I thought I would be, sitting across from my mom, drinking the hot chocolate from Ladurée, a drink so thick it reminds me of the molten chocolate they use in fondue kits. I don't remember ever drinking something so rich or delicious, and I'm almost positive that if I tested it, my spoon would stand upright in my cup. The waiter served it to us in silver pots, making me feel like Marie Antoinette. Early-in-her-reign Marie Antoinette, before the whole terrified-of-peasants-storming-Versailles thing. Ladurée hot chocolate is pure, unadulterated pre-French-Revolution-I'm-an-Austrian-princess-living-in-a-Sophia-Coppola-movie-of-excess-and-indulgence. Plus, it would be difficult to drink without a head.

"So, what's your first assignment from your grandfather?" My mom stirs a quick pour of skim milk into her black coffee. Not even in Paris will she break her diet. "Shouldn't there be something for you to work on?"

I opened Grandpa's first envelope this morning, peeling away the orange flap and ripping the metal clasp straight off in my eagerness to see what was inside. I found a handwritten letter and another, smaller envelope. Written in Grandpa's signature handwriting—all capitals, like an architect—was a message to me:

BIENVENUE À PARIS! WELCOME TO THE CITY OF LIGHTS! DO NOT OPEN YOUR ASSIGNMENT (ENCLOSED ENVELOPE) UNTIL <u>AFTER</u> YOU VISIT THE MUSÉE D'ORSAY. I'D SEND YOU TO THE LOUVRE, BUT I CAN'T STAND THOSE GHASTLY PYRAMIDS OUT FRONT.

—RP

"He wants me to visit the Musée d'Orsay. It's closed today, so I figure that's on the agenda for tomorrow. Museum in the morning, art project in the afternoon."

"He didn't want you to go to the Louvre?" she says, furrowing her brow. "See the *Mona Lisa*?"

"No, he says he prefers the Musée d'Orsay."

My mother's expression changes slightly. She signals a waiter with pockmarks on his cheeks and orders two chocolate croissants in surprisingly good French. "It's overrated," she says in a mock whisper once the waiter is out of earshot. "The *Mona Lisa*. About the size of a postage stamp. And so crowded it's impossible to get a good view."

"Yeah," I say. "I mean, I'm more excited for the Delacroix museum. And it's closed tomorrow, so Delacroix today, d'Orsay and assignment tomorrow."

My mother does the distracted nod of a person who is ready to move on to another subject. "If we have time today, I'd love to hit the Longchamp store—I'm sure they're cheaper in Paris, even if we have to convert from euros."

My face must fall, because my mom quickly backtracks. "Delacroix," she says. "Was he the one who painted ballerinas?"

"No," I answer, trying my hardest not to sound too condescending. "He did, like, horses. And harems. Things that were really exotic for the time. Like from North Africa."

My mother nods like she's trying to understand, and a small sliver of gratitude opens inside me.

The truth is, Delacroix's art isn't even what attracted me to the museum. I don't even think it holds a large collection of his paintings. But the museum is located in his former home, and it's been left almost entirely intact. Visiting Delacroix's house, I'll be able to see the windows that filled his studios with light, the counters where he left his half-open paints, the mirrors he pursed his lips in front of when he agonized over whether his work was any good. I need to see it to believe that it was real—that a real artist lived in Paris and painted real things after he brushed his teeth and made eggs for breakfast. That he's not just a name in a textbook. That I could be like him one day.

I don't explain this to my mother, who I know would immediately point out that I've been to Grandpa's house plenty of times. She won't understand that a struggling artist from Naperville, Illinois, who worked at a car dealership and painted in his basement until he quietly established a major foothold in the art scene at age fifty is very different from a bohemian soul who spent his life in Paris, focused on nothing but his art.

Not that Alice asks me anything else about Delacroix. Instead, she stares at the green streak in my hair, absentmindedly playing with the front few inches of her own hair.

"Why did you do that to your hair? Doesn't the bleaching destroy the cuticle?"

"No, I think my cuticle is perfectly healthy." I eye her hair, more auburn than it used to be but still a pretty red unlike my mousy, nondescript brown. If I had inherited my mother's hair, I probably wouldn't have dyed my own.

Alice raises her eyebrows. "At least you'll be over this"—she selects her word like it's a *macaron*—"*look* by the time you're applying for jobs."

"Probably not, because this 'look' is what I like." I take another sip of hot chocolate and let it sit on my tongue, partly to savor it and partly to keep me from saying something I'll regret later.

"I'm just saying," she starts again, "there wasn't anyone at my office—" She stops herself midsentence. I look up, and her eyes are on me. "Let's not fight this morning. We're in Paris and it's beautiful, and we should enjoy it."

"Okay," I say. And I mean it.

My mom calls over a waitress, a girl with skin that looks so perfect she doesn't even need makeup and eyelashes like a cartoon skunk. Are all French girls this pretty? Is that why fashion magazines write about them ("Eat Breakfast like a French Girl!" "The Seven Style Essentials French Girls Want You to Know!") like they're mythological creatures?

"Excuse me, is this skim?" she says, lifting up the tiny silver pitcher of milk the waitress had brought with her coffee.

"Crème," the waitress says, expressionlessly.

My mother visibly recoils. I wish I could sink into my chair and slither out the door. I wish I could move to a different table and pretend I never met the Ugly American complaining about the crème they bring for coffee.

"I need skim, please," she says and hands the confused waitress both the cream and the cup of coffee that has been ruined by an unacceptable fat content.

"Crème for the coffee," the waitress says. "Yes, milk."

"Well," my mother says, "is it milk or cream?"

The waitress looks at my mother, looks at me, then at the dairy in the tiny pitcher, then back at me. "Uh, milk?" she says. "Yes. Milk."

My mother sniffs. "See, but you said it was cream, and now I'm worried it's actually *not* milk." She hesitates for a moment and then turns back to the waitress with a fake smile. "You know what? I'll just get a cup of tea."

The waitress raises her eyebrows but takes the dishes and heads off.

"So rude," my mother says when the waitress is out of earshot.

"No, *you* were rude," I say, and then I try to backtrack. "I mean, just go with the flow. It's fine."

"If I'm paying for coffee, I want it to be the way I want it. I don't want to have to argue about whether I'm drinking milk or cream."

"Fine," I say.

I've already finished my hot chocolate by the time the tea arrives at our table. The awkwardness in the air is thicker than the richest cream you could buy in Europe.

Being in Paris makes me wonder how a place like Evanston, Illinois, even retains the will to live. How can any city dare to take up space and ink on a map when it doesn't have cobblestone streets and robin's-egg-blue roofs, or house a flurry of people too important to notice how beautiful everything is? None of the architecture in Paris has the clean, antiseptic lines of a suburb. The whole city vibrates with a density of culture and personalities that have built up, like rock sediment layering on top of itself, for centuries. An entire city block of street artists selling postcard-size paintings to tourists; a German couple affixing a lock to a bridge over the Seine; a school group giggling and shoving each other across the cobblestones; a man walking a cat on a leash. The place is pulling apart at the seams and sewing itself back together a million times a second.

I feel like Harry Potter when he goes through the brick wall behind the Leaky Cauldron and enters Diagon Alley for the first time: I wish I had better sight, better smell, better hearing, senses that haven't even been discovered yet, so that I could capture the feeling of this city in a way that won't eventually fade from my memory.

We pass a tiny bookshop, barely a full storefront, its sign a faded purple and its facade a bright blue: *La Belle Hortense*.

In the window sits a dense collection of books—some are familiar, most are not—with covers that could pass as a modern art installation. Without even venturing inside, I can imagine the smell (leather and stiff paper and Christmas trees and patchouli oil) and the countless stories that have unfolded just behind the shop's glass window. I imagine anarchists meeting, ripping out pages surreptitiously; tourists falling in love; couples hiding from the rain; lonely souls looking for sanctuary. They all exist at once in that tiny place.

I hesitate, pulled toward the store by an invisible energy.

"Do you want to go inside?" my mother asks. I do, but as I pull toward the window, I notice the lights are off and bar stools are upside down on tables like strange fairytale antlers. "It's closed," I say. "Hours are seventeen to two."

"Five P.M. to two A.M.," my mother translates.

It's a bar. A literary bar where, from the look of the counter, you pick up a new paperback and read while sipping a glass of wine. In that moment, I imagine an entirely new life for myself, where a faceless fiancé and I are regulars at La Belle Hortense, and the owner knows exactly which new releases I'll be interested in and the exact right wines with which to pair them.

"We can come back!" my mom says, and I nod. But the truth is there are some places where you don't quite belong yet. There's no place here, in this bookstore that's only open in the evenings, for Nora Parker-Holmes, the high school student from Evanston. I could walk inside, sure, but I'd be a tourist in every sense of the word. I'm not the *me* I need to be to belong in La Belle Hortense, and the realization fills me with a hollowness that I can't quite describe.

My mother and I spend the afternoon wandering and shopping. Mom takes me to Longchamp and buys me a navy blue purse that I never would have bought for myself, with a price tag that makes me a little nervous for the both of us ("It's a vacation," she says. "We're in Paris. Buy it where it'll mean something to you!").

After we walk through the chilly cavern of Notre Dame (and pick our favorite of the slack-faced gargoyles perched outside), we climb to the top of Montmartre and sit on the steps outside the white church, gazing down on the rooftops of the entire city. We're surrounded by other people—tourists, locals, students—doing the same thing, but it's still hard not to feel like we're doing something special, something singular.

"I used to come here to study," my mother says. "I'd just sit on these steps and read."

"Did you read in French?"

Mom gives me a small smile. "I was supposed to! I did buy an English translation of a Zola book I was supposed to read, I do remember that."

"Were you an English major? I didn't know you were an English major."

I try to imagine my mom, younger—not much older than I am now—her red hair in a ponytail, sitting on these very steps reading Shakespeare and Émile Zola, writing papers. It's nearly impossible to picture. The closest I can get is an image of Alice, middle-aged, sitting in a college lecture hall.

"I was a semiotics major," she says. "I don't know if those programs even exist anymore."

"I've never heard of it." I don't offer that I don't actually know what the word "semiotics" means. Instead I say, "So, what did you want to be when you grew up? I mean—"

"I wanted to be a lawyer." Her tone is matter-of-fact, but she looks at me with a sad, sideways smile.

Of course. No—Alice Parker never would have wanted to be anything that didn't involve wearing a pantsuit and black shoes that clack on linoleum floors and ordering people around. It's no wonder she's never even opened her mind to the possibility that my career could be something else.

We sit on the steps for a few more minutes while a pigeon picks at crumbs perilously close to our feet.

It's a warm summer afternoon, with a slight breeze carrying laughter and shouts from across the steps. We have an expansive view of the city beneath us like a doll set. It should be a perfect moment. I know that. But my mind keeps circling through concerns like an endless carousel: *Mom is hiding something.* Spin. *She planned to come on this trip from the beginning.*

Spin. *I bet she worked something out with Grandpa.* Spin. *What are Lena and Nick doing right now?* Spin. *Has he told her?* Spin. *I bet he told her.* Spin. *She's going to hate me.* Spin. *Mom is hiding something.* And around and around and around.

I clear my throat and check my phone. "Two thirty," I say. "The Delacroix museum closes at five—we should start heading over."

Mom stares out at Paris for a few seconds, and I wonder whether or not she heard me. Just as I'm about to repeat myself, she says, "One last place. There's one more place I want to take you quickly—just for a quick coffee. We'll be done by three and head over, plenty of time!"

"So, it's a coffee shop?"

"Sort of. It's . . . a bit of everything. I was there quite a lot when I studied here. It's on the Rue La Fayette." Her eyes search back and forth in the sky like she's trying to remember something. I can't tell whether it's a good or bad memory. "Called Le Henrique," she adds. "Hold on, let me check my phone."

She pulls me toward a shady awning to get out of the way of the steady parade of tourists. She types infuriatingly slowly, and my hands itch to take the phone from her and do it myself. It's like the Apple store teaches all parents the same terrible way to use their iPhones: *Be sure to spend at least thirty seconds on a single word. Oh, and only use one finger while you type—it'll drive your kids crazy!*

"It's not listed," she murmurs, more to herself than to me. "Maybe I'm forgetting the name. Le . . . Honorie?"

"Wait, you don't know the name? How are we supposed to know where we're going?"

"I remember where it is," my mother says.

"This better not take too long," I say. It comes out harsher than I mean it to. Impatience has a way of calcifying my words. Luckily, she spares me a response.

7

"I'M PRETTY SURE it's just around this corner," my mother says for the fourth time in twenty minutes. The sun has sunk a little, dipping behind the uneven roofs that zigzag the streets with shade, and my faith is diminishing rapidly. I'm anxious and thirsty, and my feet hurt—damn Lena and her Parisians-are-always-so-fashionable rant—because we've been walking in circles in some forgotten corner of the city, and I'm wearing ballet flats that leave angry red welts where the shoes meet my skin.

This can't possibly be a good neighborhood. The giant three-story shops housing luxury brands that I actually recognized have now been replaced by narrow jewelry stores and discount clothing shops, their windows covered by bars. Instead of women with blonde hair and linen dresses who look like they'd be on their way to a brunch regardless of the time of day, we pass skinny street punks with anarchist symbols on their ratty T-shirts and boots that look heavier than I am, and also men with potbellies wearing stained tank tops. A few of the men call out lewd comments as we walk by—even without understanding French, that tone and cadence is unmistakable—but my mother keeps an unflinchingly determined look on her face. "Le Henrique," she mumbles under her breath.

"Do you really think you would've gone to a place this far from the campus?" It's a legitimate question, but it comes out of my mouth sounding like something between a whine and an accusation.

"Yes, I do." She can't hide the hesitation in her voice.

After two more wrong turns, my mother's steps have gotten faster, verging on frantic. I try not to think about the open wounds developing on my feet.

"*Pardon*," she says to a stranger with a mustache. She approached him so quickly that I do a double take when I hear her voice. "Le Henrique? Owned by an American?"

"*Oui! Oui!*" The man is enthusiastic in the affirmative. I don't understand what he's saying, but I watch the panic drain out of my mother's face as he speaks. He talks for a while—longer than directions to a bar would merit, I can't help but think—punctuating his words with severe hand gestures.

So we set off again, down a new street that I'm sure shouldn't be there but that has somehow materialized in the last few minutes. Paris has become a twilight labyrinth. We continue making turns for a few more minutes before finding ourselves in front of a street painter we've definitely encountered before.

"This can't be right," my mom says, mostly to herself.

I check my phone for the hundredth time. "It's almost three thirty. We really need to head to the Delacroix."

My mom looks back at me as if my presence is a surprise to her. "We're almost there," she says. "And I really want you to see this place."

I brace myself. "Mom. I don't even want to go to this place, and I need to get to the museum. As it is, I'm only going to have, like, an hour there."

She gives one last look around, searching for something—a landmark, perhaps, or a sign for Le Henrique that she's hoping will magically appear on one of the shops we passed. It's the same look she had on her face when I came home from school and she told me that she and Dad needed to have "a talk" with me. I don't like seeing that face. I look around too, wondering if it's possible that Le Henrique can expand in the space between two buildings like Number 12 Grimmauld Place in *Harry Potter*. But all I see is a fishmonger and a shoe-repair store. I watch my mom for a little bit longer. Finally, she gives a resigned shrug, and we give up the search.

It doesn't take us too long to get to the Musée Delacroix. "See, we made it," my mom says. "Look, there are still some people going in now." And she's right—under a banner bearing the artist's face, a well-dressed couple make their way through the museum's entrance.

We cross the courtyard—I shuffle as fast as I can in the medieval torture devices masquerading as my shoes—and enter the museum like marathoners reaching the finish line.

"Two adults," Mom says as the man behind the desk straightens his collar.

"Ah, apologies, but we do not let patrons enter the museum with less than an hour to closing." He doesn't sound very apologetic.

"But we *just* saw two people go in," I say in a voice louder than I intended.

The man's expression doesn't change at all. "They had—'ow you say—" Another girl in a museum employee uniform steps forward. "*Re-ser-va-shuns*," she finishes for him.

"We're perfectly happy just to spend fifty minutes here," my mom says in full negotiation mode. "Please, my daughter has been dying to visit."

The man shakes his head, but I don't hear his response. I'm too busy fantasizing about using his own tie to strangle his stupid neck while the stupid girl behind him watches. She can make *re-ser-va-shuns* for the emergency room.

"Wait, hold on," I say. "I'm sure we can figure something out. Just half an hour here." Everyone goes silent; I'm not sure what I was interrupting. They look at me but say nothing. "But you're *closed* tomorrow," I say.

"*Oui*," the man says.

My mother turns to look at me, and I can tell she feels guilty. "I'm so sorry, sweetheart. Really."

I should appreciate her apology, but instead I fantasize about strangling her too.

"We came all the way to Paris," I say, the desperation in my voice palpable. "I don't know when I'm ever going to be back here again." My plea falls on deaf ears.

"Let's go." My mother tries to put her arm around my shoulder, but I duck away.

"This is *your fault!*" I say. The museum employees are listening, but I don't care. "If you hadn't attempted to relive your youth and drag me around Paris looking for a place that probably closed a decade ago, I'd be in the Delacroix museum right now."

"I know," she says. "And I've apologized. I really am very sorry."

"Why do you feel the need to control everyone and everything around you? This is *my* trip. I wanted to see this museum, but instead you *manipulated* me into following you on a wild goose chase. And now I've missed out on a great opportunity. And we're leaving Paris, and I'm never going to be able to see the Delacroix museum."

"You'll be able to come back to Paris at some point in your life," she says quietly.

"Yeah, some point in my life," I parrot back at her. "How long as it been since you came back?"

"Hey. Do not take that tone with me. I apologized. These were unlucky circumstances. We just weren't meant to visit the Musée Delpont."

The employees and I all respond in unison. "*Musée Delacroix.*" I roll my eyes and storm out of the building, my mother following close behind. "I just want to go back to the hotel, okay?" I say, swinging back around to face her. "My feet hurt from walking in circles so much."

Our cab ride back is so quiet that the driver puts on the radio. At times my mother looks over at me and takes a breath like she wants to say something, but instead she releases it in a sigh and stares out the window. I fantasize about a different version of this trip, one where I'm alone, where I went to the museum and met a tall stranger, probably a British boy studying at the Sorbonne, and we fell in love and went to La Belle Hortense together at night.

Maybe if things had gone differently today, I'd ask my mom to go back with me to the bar/bookstore this evening. But now my feet are swollen, fat baby cows in my shoes, and all I want to do is take a nap.

8

THE NEXT MORNING, I decide to leave the hotel without checking in with my mother to see if she's in the café with her coffee and a newspaper. I leave a note in the room (*Musée d'Orsay and art project*, with the word "art" underlined several times) and decide that I have fulfilled my daughterly obligations. Dinner last night (quiet, in a restaurant near the hotel) was about as friendly as the United Nations cafeteria after hostage negotiations.

But when I open the door to head out, I find myself face-to-face with my mother, her face dripping with sweat, dressed head to toe in lululemon workout clothes. Where did she even find a gym? This old boutique hotel definitely doesn't have one.

"Hi, honey," she says, wiping the sweat off her forehead and sliding past me to get into the room.

"I'm going to the museum." I point to my backpack full of art supplies for emphasis.

Her face falls. "Give me thirty minutes to hop in the shower and I'll come with you!"

But I've already started walking down the hallway toward the elevator. "I want as much time there as possible," I call out over my shoulder. "Sorry!"

If she responds, I don't hear it.

I pass a bakery, and the smell of buttery, sugary *something* makes my mouth literally water. I half-expect to be carried like a cartoon, floating horizontally, on the whiff toward the source of the smell by my nose.

Using my expert international language skills (pointing and smiling), I buy a round, curled bun with raisins in its folds. I plan on eating it while I walk, but after I take the first bite—a slight crunch into sweet, bready, crumbly paradise—I realize that the pastry deserves my respect. It's far too good to eat while I'm preoccupied with something else, even walking. So I stand outside the bakery, chewing away, feeling very grown-up, even when flakes of pastry coat the front of my dress. This is what my entire trip should be like, I think. This is freedom.

The line for the Musée d'Orsay moves quickly. "Just one?" an attendant with a heavy accent asks when I reach the velvet rope. I wonder how he knows that I'm American. "Art student?" he inquires when he sees my backpack. I nod. *I'm an art student!* It's a title I try on like a hat, and I like it a lot.

All art museums have something familiar in their DNA: sculptures in the open hall that no one knows quite how long to look at, a man with a gray ponytail and a port wine turtleneck self-consciously massaging his chin with two fingers like a caricature of an intellectual, an impossibly thin girl who sets up an easel in one of the galleries, a retirement-aged docent talking too quietly for her tour group to hear. In that way, the Musée d'Orsay is just like the Art Institute in Chicago.

Grandpa used to take me once a year, calling our house at seven fifty A.M. on a random weekday, surprising me just as I was about to leave for school.

"Call in sick, we're playing hooky," he'd say, and my mom would roll her eyes and clear her throat but oblige, and we'd go back inside and wait for Grandpa Robert's olive-green Pontiac to pull into our driveway.

"You can't keep doing this," Mom would say, tight-lipped.

"Art is an important part of her education, Al," he'd respond, winking at me. Grandpa Robert is the only person who calls my mother Al.

And then we'd be off, stopping to eat at a diner where he knew all the waitresses by their first names. Once we'd arrived at the museum, I'd always make sure we started on the second floor: the American painters exhibit. It housed my favorite paintings: *American Gothic*—always surrounded by a tour group—in one room, and in the next, *Nighthawks*, that classic scene of lonely souls sharing space (but not much else) in a diner.

And then, when I was seven, *The Reader and the Watcher*, Grandpa's most famous painting, and the only one of his in the Art Institute.

I cringe thinking back on how proud I was, or arrogant, or obnoxious—the way kids tend to be before they develop a filter—the first time I saw the painting hanging in that museum.

"Grandpa! Look!" I pointed and tugged on his windbreaker. He smiled at me. I ripped my hand from his and ran up to a stranger who was admiring the painting.

"That's my grandpa!" I said to the stranger. He was a young man, maybe thirty.

"Oh, cool."

"NO. He *painted* it! There!" I jabbed my finger dangerously close to the canvas. "That's his signature, right there. RP. Robert Parker." I then pointed at Grandpa, who probably gave an embarrassed wave.

"Hey, no way!" The young guy introduced himself—he was an art student or something—and soon, more people realized what was going on and introduced themselves as well.

"Beautiful use of negative space," one of the strangers said.

"What was it like to break out after so many years of struggling?" another asked.

"It's an honor, sir," said a woman, extending her hand.

For the rest of the visit, a whisper followed us throughout the museum. I preened like a peacock the entire time, a smirk on my face, proud to be walking next to *the* Robert Parker, but more proud that I was his granddaughter, inextricably linked to him. I was tied by my blood to one of The Greats.

Later, I asked Grandpa why he hadn't told people right away that the painting was his. If it were me, I would have declared it loudly, and probably set up a small booth signing autographs.

Grandpa swiped at his nose and crinkled his eyes, pulling me into focus. "That's not why I became a painter, bear. I painted before I became well-known, and I'll paint after no one wants to buy my work anymore."

Even now, I don't fully understand Grandpa's attitude toward his fame. I mean, I understand his love of art—the way the world slips away and time speeds up when I'm working. For me, painting feels like the way people describe yoga or their gluten-free lifestyles: It makes me feel whole. Still, I wouldn't say no to some notoriety if I got it.

To be perfectly honest, though, even more than Grandpa's success, I'm jealous of his style, the way nearly everyone in the world can see a painting of his and know instantly that it's a Robert Parker original. They recognize his distinctive lines, the way he draws noses and eyelids, how his figures are always lit from behind. Every one of my paintings, on the other hand, is filtered through the style of the last good piece I saw. I'm still searching for my identity, and I'm often afraid that I'll never find it.

Should I open Grandpa's envelope now? I have it, zipped into the same compartment in my purse as my passport. I finger its edges through the fabric. But the instructions specifically stated that I should open it *after* visiting the museum. So, with a self-satisfied sigh, I begin walking through the exhibits, hoping that I seem like a contemplative French artist/model and not a slightly jet-lagged American high school student.

I nearly jump a little when I see a painting I recognize. It's a van Gogh—I can tell from the thick brushstrokes and color palette—and it's of a church. I'm proud of myself for recognizing the artist as I check the placard to the side of the painting (*The Church at Auvers*) before feeling decidedly less proud when I realize that the painting looks familiar because it was in an episode of *Doctor Who*.

Being here, in the museum, reminds me of when I was ten and my dad and I took a road trip to the Grand Canyon while my mom was away at a conference. We drove for three days straight, staying in motels and eating drive-thru McDonald's with the conspiratorial air of criminals. ("Mom isn't around to see us get *large* fries!") Finally, on a damp morning, we drove toward a scenic lookout where a splintery wooden fence was the only thing keeping us from a steep fall.

The canyon was amazing, breathtaking, all of the adjectives people use when talking about natural wonders of the world. And then, like a director was cueing it somewhere, the clouds pulled back and revealed it was ten times bigger than we initially thought.

I was speechless. The two of us just stared for a long time, not taking our eyes off the painted orange streaks, trying to grasp just how *enormous* the thing was. That feeling of being completely overwhelmed, of insignificance in the face of greatness: That's how I feel now, in the museum.

I hover in the back of a small tour group being led by a short girl with a Scottish accent. She must be an adult—she's in a skirt and a tucked-in white button-down shirt and a floral scarf that marks her as an employee of the museum—but she doesn't look older than sixteen. How does someone have her life together that much? To come from a different country and land a job at one of the best museums in Paris at such a young age? And even if she's not actually sixteen, she's infuriatingly beautiful and probably wears sunblock every day to look so young, which means she has her shit together even more than it seemed at first glance.

Without even meaning to, I join the tour group, first skulking behind the American couple with a baby strapped to the father's chest and a group of German boys who look about fourteen and then, when I couldn't quite hear, getting bolder and coming right alongside the tour guide. She doesn't seem to mind. In fact, when I sidle up next to her, she gives me a small smile.

I miss the title of the painting, but I can see the subject matter clearly: a woman's lower body, her pelvis on display beneath a lifted sheet, her legs spread and a cloud of pubic hair in the center of the canvas. Her arms and legs are out of frame—if she weren't curled erotically she would look like the torso of a cadaver left after a serial killer.

"Obviously, when the piece was first displayed, its erotic nature caused some controversy. But the name—*L'Origine du monde*, or *The Origin of the World*—is meant to be more symbolic than sexual. Courbet features more than the woman's—uh—genitalia; he's showing us her womb, literally the source of all life. Now, this next painting was equally if not *more* controversial upon its first display . . . let's see if you can figure out why."

She gestures us toward a very different painting, a bleak scene of a woman sitting at a café table, staring down at her glass. A man sits down the bench from her, and it's not until I look closer that I realize impressionist brushstrokes give him the pallid face of a zombie clown.

"This painting was released to outrage, the type that you'd see today if Disney put out a Quentin Tarantino movie." Her pause for laughter is met only by a slight chuckle from one of the German boys. "It was shocking, to say the least," she continues, only slightly put off by the lack of audience participation. "Some said grotesque. You can see the woman's face, sullen, almost green, in line with the buffoon's face behind her. *L'Absinthe*, named for the drink before the woman, is the strong bitter beverage flavored with anise. Has anyone here had anise yet?" The American family stares blank faced, and one of the German boys raises his hand. His three companions laugh and pull it down. I can't tell what sport the jerseys they're wearing are for. "No?" the tour guide continues, looking at us. "I recommend you try it while you're here in France. Enjoy it in moderation."

I raise my hand. Slightly confused, the tour guide gestures toward me.

"You don't have to raise your hand," she says.

"Sorry, I mean, why did they think the painting was so grotesque? It looks fine." And it does. Sure, the faces are somber and slightly blurred, but it's a quiet, composed scene, a nineteenth-century French *Nighthawks*. I can't imagine pulling the curtain off a painting of a woman quietly drinking a glass of absinthe to the sound of gasps and the swoons of fainting women, too shocked to remain upright, or conscious.

"Well," she begins. The American couple move in closer, interested, until the baby gives a whimper of discomfort. Why would you even bring a baby to a museum? What could it possibly learn? I assume this is a sort of playing-Mozart-in-the-womb type of thing. The husband gives his wife a sympathetic glance and takes a few steps away, hushing the baby. The wife, who I see has a few tattoos creeping from under her tank top, moves in closer to the tour guide. "It's certainly a departure from Degas's other works, the ballerina paintings for which he's known. The scene is . . . sad. The woman is on her own, the man behind her sort of leering . . . I imagine it wasn't the type of scene the wealthy Parisians would want in their sitting rooms."

One of the German boys bumps into me, pushed by one of his laughing friends. He regains his composure, looking me up and down. "Did you pay for dees group?" he asks, waggling an eyebrow. I back away slowly, and he leaves me with a cackle, descending into anonymity among the other boys in matching jerseys.

The tour group moves on, now down to just the boys and the American woman, her husband now singing to the baby in the corner next to some Monets. I'm still staring at the painting, at the woman's face, like if I could look at her for long enough without blinking she would move and invite me to join her. She does look sad, but not like she's waiting for someone. She's content. She's where she's supposed to be, but she doesn't like it.

In my mind, I compare it to Grandpa's painting *The Reader and the Watcher*. The reader is content, while the man looking out the window is a model of impatience and anxiety. I once asked Grandpa what the story behind the painting was, who the people were, what the man was waiting for. He looked at me with his deep eyes and cleared his throat. He told me that the story is all in the painting and anything left over is supposed to be left over. I understand that looking at the woman with her glass of absinthe. I don't want to know who she is or where she came from. I just need to know that she's sad and lost in a scary place that's turned brown and abstract and grotesque around her. The painting doesn't make me want to faint; it makes me wish I were able to paint something that conveyed a twentieth of that much sadness.

Maybe I haven't been sad enough. Maybe my life has been too precious and protected in the cocoon of upper-middle-class suburbia to ever make anything worthwhile. Sure, I was sad when Dad left, but I can't help but think that it was harder on my mom. She was the one in the kitchen with the open bottle of white wine like a sitcom's depiction of the Sad Woman, the one who spent four months talking in tight sentences with a tone like a knife sharpened into a pin. I, on the other hand, saw my dad all the time. I still do—or, at least, I did. I'm not sure what will happen now that he's in Arizona and I'm college-bound.

I was sad when Nick stopped returning my text messages, and then, days later, sent a message longer than anything he'd ever sent before. But that was Taylor Swift–song sad, not artistic-existential-dread sad.

I wander the museum for a couple more hours, but I'm preoccupied. With every painting I pass, all I can think about is how much more sure the artists' brushstrokes are than my own, how much cleaner and more purposeful every one of their movements must have been. Each painting seems at once to inspire me to create something a fraction as beautiful and discourage me from even trying because I'll never match the talent on display. The awe and anxiety are still gnawing at me like a devil and angel on each of my shoulders when I leave the museum and step back into the Parisian sunlight, itching to open Grandpa's envelope. With a burst of excitement, the angel finally wins. *I get to paint something. In Paris. After visiting one of the most celebrated museums in the world.* My fingers are twitching to get started, already half-drawing the outlines of figures in my pockets.

Alice Parker might be somewhere in the city waiting for me, but it doesn't matter. I have the company of van Gogh and Degas and Courbet and Manet, and their thoughts and feelings and memories are still swirling in my brain when I step out into the sunlit street.

9

HOPE YOU ENJOYED THE MUSÉE D'ORSAY AS MUCH
AS I DID THE FIRST TIME I WENT TO PARIS AND AS
MUCH AS YOUR MOTHER DID THE FIRST TIME SHE
WENT TO PARIS. AND NOW, YOUR ASSIGNMENT:

HEAD TO THE LEFT BANK AND PICK A CAFÉ.
ORDER A CROISSANT, SIT DOWN, AND PARTAKE
IN SOME PEOPLE-WATCHING. CONTINUE DOING
THAT FOR AS LONG AS YOU NEED. WHEN YOU'RE
READY, PICK A SUBJECT AND DRAW HIM/HER.
MAKE SURE YOU'RE NOT SPOTTED. BY THE TIME
YOU ARE FINISHED, YOU SHOULD FEEL LIKE YOU
KNOW THIS PERSON.

ANY MEDIUM.

—RP

I wish Grandpa were here right now so I could squeeze his hand and show him how excited I am to get started. Just being here, in Paris, so happy to be drawing, makes me feel like I'm doing right by him. He's proud of me for everything I do, like any grandparent worth their salt: celebrating my mediocre soccer performances and B+ English papers with the kind of praise normally reserved for a Congressional Medal of Honor recipient. But I know it's my art that really makes him happy. The way the corners of his eyes crinkle when I finish a painting never fails to make me feel special and understood and loved.

But the truth is, I don't always feel like working. Sometimes I'll procrastinate for hours with a blank canvas in front of me, watching YouTube videos that I've already seen so many times I've memorized all the words. I'll wash a canvas with a background color and tell myself it needs to dry for three times longer than it actually does, during which time I will play Tetris and sing along to the *Les Mis* soundtrack alone in my room. It was so easy to put things off before I was staring, sink or swim, at the prospect of actually making art my career.

Sometimes I'll be two brushstrokes into a painting before I remember that I had an urgent appointment to make myself a snack, and then I'll conveniently forget to go back to the painting for the next four days. Inspiration feels like a temperamental housecat who shies away and pretends I don't exist when I want to cuddle her. It's usually only once I'm actually painting that inspiration creeps up behind me and rubs against my legs.

But now I'm leaving the museum feeling completely inspired. Whoever invented the museum would be so happy if he could see me now, totally fulfilling his mission. The sun is out, the sky is blue—every Electric Light Orchestra song just makes so much more sense. I'm in such a good mood that I have to wonder if it's actually because this is the first time in forty-eight hours I've been away from my mother for more than a few minutes.

Probably not.

Maybe.

Possibly.

Okay, almost definitely.

I sit in a coffee shop and look for a waitress. I plan on ordering coffee in perfect French ("Café," this version of me says, in a sexy accent, a cigarette drooping from my fingers), but when she actually approaches, I get tongue-tied and say, fully and completely in English, "Hi, can I get a coffee please and a croissant sorry thank you?"

Her face shows no sign of understanding, but she doesn't ask any follow-up questions, and a few minutes later, she returns with a tiny espresso cup balancing on a tiny saucer in one hand and a croissant in the other. She drops them at my table like it was an accident and leaves without making eye contact.

I devour half the croissant in a bite and a half, and I scan the café for a subject to draw. I'm sitting by the window, and the sunlight hits me in a strong, warm beam. I take off my cardigan and pull out my notebook as quietly as I can, trying not to be any more of a public disturbance than I already have been by being The Girl Who Spoke Loud and Obnoxious English in a French Café.

Who can I draw? There are the tween-looking girls sitting in the corner with glitter belts and headbands pulled down across their foreheads, gossiping. And then their middle-aged counterparts two tables down: two women, both in white button-downs and red lipstick, drinking wine. I could draw the businessman drinking multiple espressos and reading a newspaper, but then I see the waitress in the corner.

She's standing, looking out at the restaurant, but her eyes aren't latching onto anything in particular. It looks like she's on break, but she's not sitting, or smoking, or talking. She's just leaning in the darkest corner of the restaurant in midday, slightly hunched.

I reach into my bag to pull out charcoal, but when my fingers close around a pencil, I decide that clean, tight pencil lines are definitely a better course of action. Any concern I had about my staring being obvious fades away; the waitress is standing still and shows no signs of moving anytime soon. Her long brown hair is pulled into a high ponytail, and there's a weariness to her expression. The longer I look, the older she seems. The lines on her face jump out at me. Her entire body becomes geometry.

You know that feeling you get when you see a word so many times it stops looking like a word? Like "bowl." "Bowl" may seem like a perfectly normal word, but if you stare at it long enough, or say it enough times in your head—*bowl, bowl, bowl, bowl*—it starts to sound and look like a foreign language. That's what it feels like as I look at the waitress, then back at my drawing pad, and then at the waitress again. I watch as she becomes nothing but angles: the pitch of her elbow against her pelvis, the rhombus of light across her nose, the negative space between her legs.

When a shadow passes over my page, I swat angrily at the air around my head, hoping whatever is causing it will go away.

"'*Ello*, hi," says a voice from above me. I briefly look up to see a man with a good jawline and salt-and-pepper hair. He's smiling. "You're American, yes?" He gestures to my pad. "An artist?"

I look up at him and then look back down. "Yeah."

I can tell he's smiling from my peripheral vision. He leans down to try to see what I'm drawing, but I don't move my elbow from blocking his view, and eventually he gives up. "My friend runs a small gallery just up the avenue. Would you want to come see it?"

I remain silent as I try to get the angle of the waitress's nose just right. "I'm working," I say. And then I say nothing else. He gets the hint. Cute as he is, I'm not about to run off with some stranger in a French café, especially not when I'm so close to creating a drawing that might actually be good. No flirtation is as satisfying as the feeling of finishing a drawing exactly the way I want it. I wish Nick were here to see me, turning down a handsome French stranger. *Jesus, no, I'm not thinking of Nick now. I don't care what he sees or doesn't see.*

I briefly wonder whether Lena is still my best friend or not, whether Nick's told her and now they both hate me. The thought makes my insides twist like an empty Coke can being crushed. I push it out of my head and think only about the woman in front of me.

I sketch for the rest of her break. It can't have been longer than five minutes, but when she sighs, stretches one leg forward, and walks back toward the kitchen, I put my notebook down. My fingers ache; I didn't even realize how tightly I had been gripping the pencil.

At first I'm proud. It's a good drawing; anyone could tell you that. The waitress's limbs and features are in the right proportion, the drawing is shaded well, and it's . . . *interesting*. But the woman on the page doesn't look like the waitress. I didn't capture her sadness, her anxiety, the forlorn way she stared at nothing in particular like the girl in the absinthe painting.

My first instinct is to tear the page up—to rip it out of my notebook and then into as many tiny pieces as I can manage, covering the café floor with paper snow. But it is a good drawing. It may not be right, but it is good.

I think about my grandpa's note. *Do I feel like I know her?* From my drawing, this is who I imagine she is: She's in her mid-thirties, living with a man name Jean-Claude who works as a tour guide and can't commit himself to marriage. He cheated once, long ago, and though he swore he's reformed, she's still nervous, waiting tables more nights than she lets on and putting money away into a saving account that's just for her, just in case. She's worked at this café long enough that they've offered her a promotion, but she's always refused. She has a cat named something hilariously human, like Charles or Frank, but she doesn't see what's funny about it. And she's not happy. Not sad, not most of the time, but not happy. This is what I extrapolate from my drawing.

This woman never would have kept hooking up with Nick after he told her he didn't want his friends to find out, after he told her he "didn't want it to be a whole thing." This a woman who knows who she is.

I look back at the drawing. She looks so much lonelier than I had intended. Maybe I can make it better when I get back to the hotel, before bed. I check my phone, and it's almost five o'clock. I'm surprised I haven't heard from my mom yet, especially about dinner.

I make it back to the hotel so easily that I feel like a Parisian local, or at least the type of American who goes to Paris so often that she has restaurant recommendations and knows store workers by their first names. *I am a competent lady artist! A brilliant world traveler!* Even if I do accidentally say "good morning" instead of "good evening" to the French doorman who lets me inside the hotel.

I hesitate at the door to our room, not sure whether it feels right to burst in victoriously or to plan to apologize for ditching Mom all day. More than anything, I just want to plop on the bed, face down, until dinner. But then I hear a voice— her voice—in a harsh whisper on the phone. Hesitantly, I slip inside the room.

"No, no, I appreciate the help. Really. It's just—no, okay. Okay. That's fine." Her eyes meet mine. She looks both furious and terrified. "My daughter just walked through the door. We'll have to continue this conversation another time," she says before hanging up the phone.

"Hi!" she says to me, a little too sharply, with the ringing sound of the phone slammed into its holster still vibrating in the room. "How was your day?"

"It was great," I say, but the tension in the room drains any actual excitement I may have had. "Went to the museum, drew a little." I say the words like they're lines in a play. I want to ask what the phone call was about, but I know she'll just say, "Work."

"That's it? 'Went to the museum, drew a little'? I asked you how your day in Paris was!" Her voice is getting louder. I'm already sitting on the bed.

I try to cut her off. "I just meant—"

"Yes, I know what you 'just meant.' I hope you had a wonderful day."

"Okay, I don't understand why you're getting so angry."

"I'm not getting angry," she says, fixing her watch, which has come unfastened.

"Okay then," I say.

She looks at me with tight lips and then pulls on one of her boots. "I'm going out to dinner. You're welcome to join me."

"No," I say, relishing the fact that I don't have to play nice. "I'm fine, thanks."

She laces up her boots and pulls on a scarf. "Fine," she says. "Good night."

The room feels oddly quiet with her gone. I turn the TV to the only English channel I can find (CNN) and try to fix the drawing for Grandpa, but I'm pretty sure I only make it worse. I decide to just mail it as is.

I eat dinner alone in the hotel room (rice and meat called "doner kebab" that I bought from a hole-in-the-wall restaurant on the corner) and fall asleep before my mother is back. We're leaving for Belgium tomorrow morning. Hopefully it won't be a disaster.

And almost immediately, it's a disaster.

"Please explain to me why we needed to get to the train station *four hours early*?" My mother is contentedly sitting on a plastic seat and reading the *Atlantic* while I slowly die of boredom.

"I didn't want us to miss the train," she says, licking her thumb and then turning the page. What a disgusting thing. Why do adults always do that?

I sigh, and when my mom doesn't notice, I sigh louder. Still no reply. We already checked out of our hotel and took two buses to get to the train terminal on the outskirts of Paris, so there is absolutely nowhere to go. Not to mention that I have my carry-on to deal with, so even if I wanted to explore, I'd be weaving through the sidewalks with an electric-green turtle-shell-shaped suitcase. And so I sigh again.

I've already finished my book, so all that's left to do is wander up and down the train station, examining the stale candies in a vending machine that looks like it hasn't had a patron in at least a decade and looking at the signs for all the other places the trains are headed to.

"How do you know this is even the right train?" I say to my mom from a few rows of seats away. "It says AMSTERDAM on the electronic screen."

She glances up from a book she opened after finishing her magazine, and for half a second I think she's going to become concerned, but then her face relaxes back into full confidence, the look I've seen her give in a courtroom on days she couldn't find a babysitter for me.

"This is the three P.M. train. It stops in Brussels, but I assume it continues on to Amsterdam," she says.

"Okay," I say. "But it looks like there are, like, four trains leaving at three P.M. How do we know which one stops in Brussels?"

And now she sighs like *I'm* the one who made the train station confusing. I wish there were more people here—someone we could ask or try to commiserate with about this confusion. But the station—or at least the distant corner of the station we're in—stays relatively empty until two fifty-six (or, as the big electric clock says in military time, fourteen fifty-six), when a wheezing, exhaling metal tube of a train crawls into the terminal and, with a tinny shiver, opens its doors.

We go from sitting in the plastic chairs of the train station under fluorescent lighting to sitting in the dusty plush seats of the train in the semi-darkness of a compartment shared only with an elderly couple who smell like canned soup.

I have nothing to do but listen to music and watch my iPhone battery slowly go to red while I sketch, although my options for subjects are limited. There's the terrible '80s pattern of the seats, the luggage rack, or the view out the train window, which, at the moment, is a dingy train station.

"Would you *please* stop tapping your leg?" my mother half-whispers to me, clearly trying not to bother the nice elderly couple. I can tell they're French. The woman is wearing a scarf and has blood-red nails on her gnarled hands, and the man is in a fedora that somehow doesn't look ridiculous.

I didn't even notice I was doing it, but it's the only thing keeping me from going stir-crazy. I've been sitting for longer than I want to think about. I do try to stop, at least for a few minutes, but when it starts up again it's not my fault—it's just my body trying not to deteriorate like the muscles of an astronaut on the International Space Station.

"Can I have that book you brought?" I say, gesturing to the paperback on my mom's lap. It's a thriller, about a woman and an affair and a train and a secret identity. I think I read that Reese Witherspoon is adapting it into a movie.

My mother licks her thumb and flicks the page of her magazine. "I'm going to read it when I finish with this magazine," she says.

I start bouncing my leg again, half in protest and half because I literally have nothing else to do. "You're not even reading it," I say.

I realize that was a mistake as soon as my mother puts down the magazine and turns to face me, her eyes cold and dark like a shark.

"You were acting like a *brat* in Paris, and I'd appreciate it if you showed a little respect now. Show a little gratitude."

Why do parents say "brat" when they really mean "bitch"? I bounce my leg as hard as I can and look her dead in the eye. "Excuse me. Grandpa is the one who gave me this trip, and you're the one tagging along."

At this point, the elderly French couple sharing the train compartment with us exchange a glance that I know means, "Typical—ugly Americans, thinking the whole train compartment belongs to them," and obviously I'm embarrassed, but I can't stop myself. I can't just turn this into a good mood.

My mother places her hand on my knee, hard, and she hisses out, "*Could you PLEASE contain yourself.*"

"*Fine,*" I hiss, keeping my leg as still as I can. Now my mom sighs.

"Nora, I apologize. I came on this trip to bond with you, not to fall back into old habits. So tell me: How are things with Lena?"

Lena? Is she really asking me how things are with Lena, now? What am I supposed to say? *Well, Mom, I was hooking up with this guy who didn't care about me, and then Lena asked if she could maybe go for it because she thought we had only hooked up the one time, and instead of telling her that she shouldn't "go for it" because her "going for it" would feel like a thousand tiny needles in my heart, I instead said, "Sure, go ahead," and now they're dating and just fabulously happy together.*

"She's fine. I don't know. Back in Evanston."

"Honestly, I can't see how you expect us to get to know each other better if you're not going to open up."

I straighten my back. "*Me*, open up? How about that phone call that you're obviously lying to me about?"

"'Lying' is a *very* strong word, Nora," she says in her I'm-about-to-take-away-your-car-privileges voice.

"Oh, I'm sorry, what word would you like me to use?"

And I swear, without even saying anything to each other, the old couple gather up their bags and leave the compartment, giving us death glares as they make their way out.

I slide across the bench so I'm as physically far from Alice Parker as I can be. *Of course* we've turned into the ugly Americans who can't even ride a train without ruining it for ourselves and everyone around us. Go big or go home, right?

10

Dear Lena,

Belgium is a disaster. Like, slapstick-comedy-about-a-family-Thanksgiving disaster. Already, Belgium is the equivalent to setting a turkey on fire and accidentally baking someone's diamond earrings in the stuffing. It doesn't help that I've gained about 17.5 million pounds from eating croissants. Luckily, I'll lose as many pounds when I go to England. (Because it's money! Do you get it? Do you miss my sense of humor?)

I'm writing you from the hotel that we finally found after definitely getting on the wrong tram, probably accidentally not paying, and then getting off at a stop a full half hour's walk from the hotel. The trams here have no clear signage explaining where you're supposed to put the ticket! The doors just open and close automatically, and people step on and off. And all of their automatic ticket stands are completely in French.

Mom and I bickered the whole way to our hotel, which turned out to be a shriveled gray building on the world's dirtiest river. There is literally a plastic lawn chair hanging from a telephone line visible from my window. We haven't gotten to the city center yet, but my impression of Brussels is gray, dirty, bleak, and filled with passive aggression. The only thing getting me through this is the promise of tomorrow's day trip to Ghent to see the altarpiece, which is supposed to be life-changing. Which is a good thing, because right now I would be in favor of my life being changed.

I came here because I wanted to feel independent, but I feel more like a child than ever. And it doesn't help that I don't know any French, so really my mom is the only person I can talk to if I even want to talk. If I had been traveling alone, I would be staying in a hostel with other young people. We'd hang out and go on pub crawls and become friends for life, friends you see in beer commercials and ads for tampons, running along beaches in bikinis and dancing through the night around a bonfire or something.

Instead, I'm in hotels, walking on eggshells around Alice Parker.

Sorry for being such a depressive mope. I've been doing really good drawings here, and I'm excited to finally get to the program in Ireland. Hope you're well, and hope you're still good with Nick. Tell your sisters I say hi and that they shouldn't watch *Hocus Pocus* until I'm back with you and the entire Peyson clan.

Love love love,
Nora

I wake up early, expecting to have a few minutes to myself, but my mom is already lacing up her gray gym shoes. I think the brand is Nike Obvious Tourist.

"What's the plan, Stan?" she says with more energy than I would assume is possible before ten A.M. and/or several very strong cups of coffee. Clearly trying to turn the other cheek from our train-car-evacuating argument on the way here.

"I was going to go to the city center and do Grandpa's assignment."

"Great!" she says with enthusiasm that has to be fake. "Let's walk down together. I'll check out some of the chocolate shops and buy you a waffle when you're done."

She's too polite. She's treating me like a college roommate whom you secretly suspect of stealing your stuff when you leave the room.

Following the map they gave us at the front desk, we cross the dirty river. The architecture of the buildings seems to change with every block, like we're walking through a museum diorama instead of a city. Discount shoe stores and places selling seafood that look like they haven't been renovated since 1992 become cheap hair salons and tacky dive bars, then become cell phone stores and McDonald's, followed by pharmacies and bakeries and buildings that look lifted from the eighteenth century. In three city blocks we seem to have journeyed from Detroit to the little French town from *Beauty and the Beast*. I look at the assignment Grandpa gave me.

THE TOWN HALL WAS BUILT BY MULTIPLE BUILDERS AT ONCE, ALL CONCERNED WITH SPEED AND SAVING MONEY. LEGEND HAS IT THAT WHEN THE ARCHITECT WHO DESIGNED THE BUILDING FINALLY SAW HIS NOW-COMPLETED PROJECT, HE CLIMBED TO THE TOP OF THE TALLEST TOWER, SURVEYED THE CITY, AND LEAPED TO HIS DEATH.

EXAMINE THE BUILDING. DISCOVER WHY THE ARCHITECT WAS FILLED WITH SUCH DEEP DESPAIR. DRAW THE BUILDING AS PRECISELY AS YOU CAN. DETAILS CAN BE A MATTER OF LIFE AND DEATH.

—RP

He included a tiny dollar-store protractor, most likely to help me get my angles right. I don't say anything out loud, because there's no way my mom will understand, but I'm kind of terrified. I worry that, even trying as hard as I can, I'll end up with a tangle of lines that doesn't resemble anything good. Straight lines and perspective are a bit of a weakness for me, and when I say "weakness," I mean "total blind spot." Even in elementary school art class, teachers criticized my "chicken scratch" style, despite the fact that my pieces were clearly the best. The trend continued through middle school, high school, after-school lessons at the Community Center, and summer programs. All short lines. I don't do heavy, black, straight. I'm good at all over the place and impressionistic, lines layered on top of each other until they come out looking like real art, the type that would be at home hanging alongside Robert Parker's in the Art Institute. Even when I draw faces—my specialty—I leave the shadow of the shapes I sketched for guidance. Drawing a building isn't going to make me look like a real artist.

Following a little map I picked up on a street corner, my mother and I walk together toward the town hall. I swear there's a chocolate shop every second storefront. This isn't hyperbole. Literally, we walk, pass a gourmet-looking chocolate shop with towers of dipped marshmallows and toffee tilting in the windows, walk another four steps, and there's another, this one with onyx lettering and a luxury salon feel, with each piece of chocolate under its own glass dome.

"How could any economy possibly support this many chocolate shops?"

"Tourists," my mother replies simply.

"I was kidding."

Her pace doesn't slow. We turn into one of the stores. "Oh," she says. "Ha, yes."

"Having to explain a joke ruins it," I say. "It's like that old saying—you know, something like 'explaining a joke is like dissecting a frog: You'll understand it, but you'll have a dead frog.'"

"Do you think your aunt Jocelyn would like these?" My mother holds up a box of dark chocolates shaped like flower blossoms.

"You weren't even listening to me. I was explaining a comedy thing."

"I was—dead frog. Maybe she prefers white chocolate?"

Even though the town center is full of gorgeous Gothic buildings, the town hall is still easy to spot. It's almost the full length of the entire city block, so tall I can't capture it in an Instagram square, and dotted with hundreds of tiny windows. Just thinking about the windows makes my stomach sink.

With her chocolate purchased (a thoughtful combination of dark AND white), my mom decides to duck into a Starbucks on a nearby corner. "I'm going to send a few e-mails, for work, with their WiFi," she says, gesturing with her head. "Why don't you get started drawing? And meet me over here when you're done?"

"Well I don't know how long it'll take—"

"That's fine," she says, looking distracted. "I'll be right over here."

And so even though at this moment I would rather do

literally anything else, I nod and smile, pretending to be excited. "Sounds good."

Forty-five minutes in, and my drawing is already a lopsided Tim Burton excuse for an architecture sketch. Even using the protractor, my angles are somehow slightly too wide, and trying to draw straight lines using the six-inch ruler at the bottom means that the base of the building is only straight in six-inch increments. And no matter how many times I swear I counted the windows on each side of the building, I can't seem to get the number right. If I hadn't already cramped every muscle in my hand drawing half a million tiny square windows I would have ripped the page off my notepad and started over.

I've been staring at this building for so long that the windows have all blurred into tiny, shapeless glass blobs. I look up and see that the windows are two panes across with a block below them. I look down, I look up again, and now they're one pane across. Then I draw that and look up again, and it turns out they *are* two panes across but without the block, and I need to erase like a maniac and start over. I'm starting to understand why van Gogh cut off his ear. And shot himself.

I have no read on how much time has passed, but it's been at least long enough for three distinct tour groups to meet in the main square under the giant orange umbrella, hear the same cheesy introduction, and depart.

I'm struggling with getting the shape of the tower right when I hear my mother's voice.

"How's it going?"

I quickly block as much of the terrible, smudged disaster of a pencil drawing behind me as I can.

"Fine," I say.

"Interesting building." She's not looking at my drawing at all. "Did you notice how the tower is off-center? And look," she points. "Even the arch *in* the tower is off-center. Someone's head probably rolled for that."

I laugh. I can't help it. I start laughing so loud Belgium strangers probably think I'm having a nervous breakdown.

I look down at my drawing, and suddenly it doesn't look so bad. "I think I might be done," I say.

"Looks really good!" she says, examining the drawing a little closer than I'd like. "So how about we try one of these famous waffles?"

I do not have the poetry of language to describe how delicious this waffle is.

It's about six inches across, definitely not the plate-sized "Belgian waffles" they serve at breakfast places in the States. They serve them in these little cardboard boats, like how they'd serve hotdogs at a baseball game. The waffle is chewy and dense and almost gritty with sugar. It's warm and heavy with Nutella and strawberry slivers (Mom chose just whipped cream). It's like the best doughnut I've ever had, if the doughnut made love to a crepe and ran away to have its baby. I want about seven more.

"Save some room for fries," my mom says when she sees me edging back toward the stand, where they are tossing fresh rounds of dough onto the press with a smell so good I could float on it like a cartoon character.

I could pretend that we wait at least an hour post-waffle to have fries, but I would be completely lying. We go directly toward the longest line (the shop we overheard several tour guides point out as the best fry shop in Brussels) and each get an order, with our own sides of spicy mayo. By the time we finish the hot, crispy, greasy things, their cardboard carriers are transparent.

"Did you know," my mom says, her fingers tracing the bottom of her dish for the crispy burnt bits, "that 'French fries' is actually a misnomer? They were invented in Belgium, and during World War I . . . World War II? Anyway, during one of the wars, Americans saw them eating them in Flanders but assumed since the Belgians were speaking French that they were in France. Hence," she waggles the last burnt bit, "French fries."

"That's actually pretty cool," I say, just beginning to feel all of the grease I consumed in the previous hour settling in my stomach. "How'd you know that?"

"Heard half a tour while I was waiting for you to do your little drawing."

The phrase "little drawing," the dripping condescension hidden within those four syllables, immediately freezes any goodwill I was feeling. My face stiffens into a frown, and I feel the grease so heavily now I worry that I'm going to be sick.

"So what do you want to do for the rest of the day?" my mother asks, patting her stomach. It's one P.M.

I contemplate the silent treatment, but the idea of having another fight with Alice Parker is too exhausting to consider.

So I swallow my frustration whole. "We could go to the Hergé museum? The cartoonist who did Tintin?" It's the only thing I can think of, since we've already walked past a lifetime's worth of gourmet chocolate shops, eaten a waffle and an order of fries each, and passed the famous *Manneken Pis* sculpture. The list of Brussels "must-see" attractions is getting smaller by the minute.

"Sure, I used to love Tintin," she says.

I've actually never read a Tintin book. But I know the art and style, and I read the Wikipedia page this morning, so I can discuss it like I know what I'm talking about. It's a little disheartening to think that my mom is more knowledgeable than me about something relating to art.

We spend fifteen minutes walking there—practically rolling ourselves after the sheer quantity of fried food we put in our bodies—in silence. It's obvious even without looking at a map when we finally find the museum; the entire side of the building is painted with Tintin, his iconic round face and butter-yellow hair. I already feel a little better just thinking about going to a museum filled with cartoons.

"Closed," my mom says. A sign is posted on the door. "It's closed today. Open tomorrow, though."

"Tomorrow we're going on the trip to Ghent." I'm practically shouting.

"Well, fine," she says, sputtering. "*I* didn't plan the schedule."

"I KNOW!" I shout back. I'm mad at myself. Mad for not planning what we would do in Brussels, mad that I didn't check the opening hours for museums I wanted to visit, mad that I drove myself crazy drawing the town hall without realizing it was off-center. Mostly I'm mad that this is my one chance for a European adventure and my mother and I are both ruining it at every turn.

"Well," she says crisply, "is there anything else you wanted to see while you were here? What would you be doing if you were alone?"

"I don't know." I check the list of tourist attractions: a military museum, a finance museum, a beer tour—nothing that excites me at all. "There's, like, nothing to do in this city."

We end up walking back to the hotel, back past the McDonald's and the seafood shops and the discount shoe stores, across the dirty river. We spend the rest of the afternoon on our laptops taking advantage of free WiFi and the mutual decision not to speak. The dynamic feels better than in Paris, though. Less hostile. My mother and I have actually become an unlikely team, united allies against the awful city that is Brussels. *The enemy of my enemy* and all that.

Later that night, I'm suddenly struck by the distinct paranoia that when Lena gets my letter, she's going to open it with Nick, and they're going to read it together and laugh. The thought is crazy—delusional, even—but it plays in my head like a distorted nightmare. I remember hearing in English class about Caroline Lamb, who fell madly in love with Lord Byron and then fell madly insane when he broke off their relationship. She would write him long love letters, including a lock of her hair, asking for a lock of his back. Lord Byron, cad that he was, was dating someone else, and he and the little so-and-so would read poor Caroline's letter and laugh, even going so far as to send back a lock of his new girlfriend's pubic hair, pretending it was from Byron's head, because the color and texture were similar enough, which is just about the most horrible and heartbreaking thing I can think of. (They didn't tell us the pubic-hair part in class; I looked it up afterward online.) It's not that I'm still in love with Nick—I'm not, obviously, and I never was, obviously. But I will say I feel like I have a lot in common with Caroline Lamb at the moment.

I definitely don't tell my mom, who doesn't understand boys or friends or English poets of the romantic period. We just keep each other company like mutually polite roommates at this point, and that's fine.

11

"YOU NEED YOUR tickets."

The woman at the tour-company counter has her hair in a beehive, like the housewife in a *Far Side* cartoon. She's typing slowly, barely looking at us. She is the oldest person I've ever seen with fake nails.

"We have our tickets," I say, showing my iPhone screen again. "See? Confirmation e-mail, receipt, tickets."

The *Far Side* cartoon glances at my phone, then immediately back to her far more fascinating computer screen. "Your tickets need to be in hard copy."

My mom steps in. "It doesn't say *anywhere* that the tickets need to be hard copy."

Far Side heaves a sigh like she's Atlas himself and reaches a wizened arm to snatch the phone from my hand. It took us forty minutes to find the Belgian Adventure offices tucked into a far corner of the city, on a street that wasn't labeled on the map, where the e-mail had told us to meet the group at eight A.M. sharp.

"Mmm," she says. "This tour doesn't run today."

Mom takes control, stepping slightly in front of me like a human shield. "We bought and paid for these tickets, which were available online . . ." She trails off, the staccato in her voice draining away when she realizes her words are having exactly zero effect on the woman behind the counter.

I notice a small group hovering outside and grab my mom's hand to pull her with me.

A handsome guy who looks to be in his late twenties approaches us. "You guys have tickets for the Ghent thing today too?" He's Australian. He's joined by his girlfriend or wife, who is beautiful with long dark hair and bangs.

"The customer service here is a disaster," she adds. "Never using Belgian Adventure again."

"Yeah," the guy continues. "We had mates who came to Belgium and went on the tour to Ghent and said it was un-missable."

"I just wanted to see the altarpiece," I say. Maybe it's something about how friendly they are, or how we're all in the same sinking boat, but it's surprisingly easy to talk to them, and normally I hate talking to strangers.

"What altarpiece?"

"The *Ghent Altarpiece*. It's one of the most important

masterpieces of the Northern Renaissance. Fifteenth century, I think. It's a cornerstone of Christian art. Sometimes they call it *The Adoration of the Mystic Lamb*, probably painted by Jan van Eyck."

All three of them—the two Australians and my mom—listen intently, and I immediately realize that I haven't told her anything about the altarpiece yet.

"Yeah, yeah," the girlfriend says. "I've heard of that. It's a big deal!" She turns to the guy. "Jan van Eyck's the guy who did the *Arnolfini Portrait* painting."

"Oh, no way, that's so nice. Lucky you guys are on our tour; we'd have totally missed that. Where is it?"

"The Saint Bavo Cathedral," I say. "Don't worry, it's definitely part of this tour."

"*If* this tour happens," my mother says, and the three of us turn to look at the *Far Side* lady again.

The guy gestures his head toward the tour offices. "This is a fucking shit-show. Oh, shit—" He covers his mouth with his hands. "Sorry for the foul language."

"Don't worry," I say. "I swear all the fucking time." He and his girlfriend both laugh, and I resolve not to make eye contact with my mom for at least twenty minutes.

A small cluster of people forms around a woman who is about four feet tall with a tuft of white hair like a decorative poodle. "The tour for Ghent?" she wheezes. There's a murmur of approval. "Hand over your tickets and follow me to the bus."

"Excuse me," I say. "I didn't print the tickets, but I have them on my phone?"

"You need the tickets printed," she replies, taking other people's responsibly printed-out pages, not looking at me.

"Yeah, but I didn't know that." My mom comes up behind me for backup.

"It doesn't say anywhere that the ticket needs to be printed out."

The woman heaves a heavy sigh and gestures for me to give her my ticket. "Fine," she says, looking at it. "Follow me!"

"It's like she's doing us a favor," my mom says to me as we walk toward the parking lot. "We paid for this."

After we file onto the bus, the tiny tour guide informs us that her name is Elsa, and "Would you please take these headphones and plug them into the seat for the audio tour to begin?" We acquiesce. As soon as the bus starts moving, the "tour" scratches to life with a '90s-sounding electronic theme song.

Turns out, the audio tour is a prerecorded, heavily accented voice just naming buildings as we pass them: "City hall. Former beer hall. The Ludwig Building. The National Bank." No context, no history, and subpar audio quality. And since the tour was prerecorded, the timing is a little off. "Actually, *that's* the National Bank," Elsa adds at one point, gesturing vaguely toward a turreted building down the block.

"This," I say to my mom, "is the worst tour in the history of tours."

"They should give tours commemorating how terrible this tour is."

"A bust of Elsa."

"A statue of the woman at the tour-company counter."

"She already is a statue."

We erupt in laughter, together, for the first time since I can remember.

"Excuse me," a man with a bucket hat leans across the aisle toward us. "I'm trying to listen here."

My mom disguises her smile. "Very sorry."

Elsa interjects the audio tour with random musings on Brussels, where we've been informed that she's lived with her second husband for four months. "A family friend used to live there," she says, gesturing toward an apartment building, drowning out the sound of the audio tour, pointing out the public gardens that are still several blocks away.

"I think I'm going to try to fall asleep," I say and rest my head on the bouncing, vibrating bus window, letting the sound of Elsa and the electronic tour lull me into sleep like the world's laziest lullaby.

"Nora." My mom shakes me, and for a moment I'm sure we're there already, although in my half-awake delirium I can't remember exactly where *there* is. "Nora. I think she said the cathedral is closed."

"Hm?"

"The woman. I think she said the cathedral is closed today. Preparing for a festival or something? Saint Pavel's?"

"That's the festival?"

"No, the name of the cathedral. That's the name of the one with the altarpiece you wanted to see, right?"

"Saint Bavo."

"I think she said it was closed!"

I'm starting to wake up now. "That can't be true. I bet they wouldn't have even run the tour today. Or they at least would have told us before we got on the bus."

"I could've sworn . . ."

"Why would they close a cathedral? Cathedrals don't close, do they?"

"You're asking me?" Two suburban half-Jewish agnostics are not the appropriate source for insight into the business hours of cathedrals.

We sit in uncomfortable silence for the rest of the ride. I half-attempt to fall back asleep, but I'm waiting for the chance to ask Elsa or Enda or whatever her name is whether or not the one thing I wanted to see in Belgium is even open.

The bus finally pulls into a dusty parking lot and squawks into park. As we descend the steps, I make a beeline for the tour guide and tap her on the shoulder.

"Excuse me? While we were on the bus, did you mention that Saint Bavo Cathedral is closed today?"

"Military wedding," she says, counting the rest of the descending tourists.

"But what about the altarpiece? How are we going to see it?"

"Can't see it today. I said so on the bus."

The Australian couple from before has made their way

beside me, equally incised. "Yeah, but why wouldn't you tell us that before we boarded the bus? Maybe we would have gone on the tour a different day."

Elsa gestures to a walkie-talkie the size of an ostrich egg. "Just found out while we were driving." With that, she walks away, carrying a sparkly baton that looks like a children's toy, which she uses to lead the group as we make our way into town.

I shake my head. "How is this company real? How is this woman a tour guide?"

My mother laughs. Genuinely. "I'm assuming the European training system leaves a little to be desired. But look!" She points toward a tower that even I have to admit is pretty picturesque.

"It's nice," I agree. And then we nod, wondering what else there is to do in this city. Turns out, not a lot. We pass the nice clock tower, but as we get closer, our view is obstructed by hanging beams and ropes for a stage that's going to be erected at night ("For the festival," Elsa informs us know-ingly). We pass approximately seven hundred chocolate shops. I have to imagine somewhere there's a good Ghent, a Ghent where tourists in the know would be welcomed into tiny European speakeasies and discuss art and literature with handsome men named Claude while sipping cocktails with names no one can pronounce. I'm sure somewhere there's a charming courtyard with a restaurant where the waiters know every customer by first name, and when tourists come in they offer the chef's best dish, on the house. I can imagine an alternate universe where Ghent is a beautiful, interesting, culturally rich town. But that's not the universe this tour company dropped us off in.

After Elsa herds us back to a pocket off the main square, she waggles her baton once more in the air for good measure. "Be back here in forty-five minutes. The bus is leaving. Or else you'll find your own way back."

My mom and I, the Australian couple, and oddly enough the man with the bucket hat find ourselves sitting at the only semi-decent café we can find. Bucket Hat orders a beer. The rest of us order cappuccinos.

"Shame about the altarpiece," Bucket Hat says after taking his first swig of beer.

The Australian couple light up. "Yes! You knew about it too? It's well-known, right?" They seem particularly vindicated by the idea that the altarpiece is something more people have heard of than just me. Their suspicions have been confirmed that it's not, as Elsa put it, "just a painting."

"Yeah," Bucket Hat continues. "It's the only reason I took this tour to Ghent in the first place."

"Us too!" I exclaim. "And now there's, what, a wedding or something? We should just crash it."

The Australians laugh. Bucket Hat doesn't. "Do you think we'd get in trouble?" he says.

"Oh," I say. "Yeah. No, I was kidding. We'd definitely get in trouble, right?"

The subject is dropped, and the bill is paid. Our little group scatters off to collect some last-minute photographs or chocolate purchases, as the case may be.

We're already headed back toward the bus when my mom tugs at the bottom of my shirt. "Hey," she whispers. "Let's go."

I turn toward her. "To the buses?"

"No!" She looks around and lowers her voice even more. "To the church. The cathedral. Let's . . . check it out."

"You're not serious."

"Come on! Let's try."

And before I know what's happening, I'm following my mother down a narrow cobblestone alley beside the cathedral, looking for a way in. Through one of the windows, I see men in military dress filing into pews alongside women in giant hats. They seem to be just milling about, but I can't tell if the ceremony is over or if it hasn't even begun yet.

Mom points to a small, unobtrusive wooden door being held open by a stopper. "Come on," she says.

My heart is pounding. I'm light-headed. I've never done anything like this before, let alone with my mother. We weave through a dark room, the sound of our footsteps eclipsed by the echoing of casual chatter from the main hall. It looks like we're in some sort of classroom, with a few scattered tables and a small chalkboard.

"We just have to look like we belong," my mom says. I almost snort laughing. We're both wearing yoga pants and gym shoes.

"At least take off your fanny pack," I say. She does, and I shove it into my backpack. I can hear the sounds of conversation, louder, just on the other side of the door. "On the count of three. One, two . . ." On three, I pull open the door, which makes an excruciatingly loud creak, and we both slide through.

The good news is, no one seems to notice us. The place is milling with wedding guests in formal wear, but also people setting up tables and taking coats. It's crowded enough that two extra bodies don't immediately draw attention.

The bad news is that I don't see the altarpiece anywhere. In my imagination, it's giant—the centerpiece of the cathedral— and lit up, maybe with neon arrows pointing to it. Maybe I got the wrong cathedral. Or the wrong town. Maybe I made up the entire concept of an altarpiece altogether. Maybe—

"Look," my mom half-whispers, directing my attention toward the corner of the cathedral, where, blocked off by a small metal barrier, sits the altarpiece. We move together, silently as ghosts, turning every few steps to make sure no one has noticed our presence. Luckily, it seems like most people's attention has been diverted by the entrance of a very old man— flanked by a few soldiers with sashes and swords—who seems pretty important.

"It's beautiful," my mother whispers, and it is. The colors are muted, but the intricacy of it is breathtaking. A lot of religious altarpieces, at least the ones they showed us in AP art history, look weirdly flat, with babies with abs and faces like adults. But this is stunning. It's better than the photographs.

The lights change, and without our noticing, it seems like most people have taken their seats. We're standing behind the pews, with a good view straight up the aisle to where the priest is standing. He's making direct eye contact with me.

I tug on my mom's coat sleeve. "Do you think we should—"

A wedding march begins to play, and everyone turns to look at the back of the cathedral, expecting to see the wedding party making their way up the aisle. Instead, their eyes find us: two Chicago suburbanites with one backpack and one fanny pack between them, and two panicked expressions. Out of the corner of my eye, I see the groom in full military regalia begin walking out toward the aisle, eyeing us the entire time. I desperately scan the building for possible exits.

A woman with a tight updo approaches us and begins half-whispering, half-yelling in rapid French or maybe Dutch; I'm too nervous to care or notice. My mom and I whip across the cathedral and out the wooden door we entered through, making our way into the classroom and finding ourselves face-to-face with the bride, her father, and two other women.

"Congratulations," I shout as we fly out the door and into the sunlight, onto a street that still exists, everything familiar and foreign and beautiful all at once. Adrenaline has made the world Claritin-ad sharp.

We scan the horizon for Elsa's sparkling stick, find it, and rejoin the group without anyone commenting on our tardiness. We pass under Elsa's baton, giggling like escaped convicts (do escaped convicts giggle?). We discuss it in play-by-play the entire way home. *Remember how we just walked in? Did you see the look on the groom's face? I can't believe you said, "Congratulations!"*

Everyone else on the bus shoots us odd glances, jealous that they weren't a part of whatever is making us so happy.

We're still floating by the time we make it to the hotel.

"I can't believe we did that," I say, collapsing onto the bed.

"I'm glad we got to see the altarpiece!" Mom calls from the bathroom. She is flossing. I suddenly feel a wave of gratitude that my mom is here, that I didn't have to suffer through the world's worst tour alone. I smile into the comforter. "Thank you for sharing that with me," she says, entering the room.

I almost say, "Thank you for coming," but I catch myself. "You're welcome. I'm glad we did it."

She sits down on the corner of my bed. "I'm going to miss you next year," she says, looking at the floor. I get the impression that if she looks at me she might begin to cry. "The house has just been so quiet since—you know." She means since Dad left. "It gets lonely sometimes."

"I know," I say.

"You do?" she says, surprised.

"I mean, yeah. The . . ." I hesitate. "The crying . . ."

"I thought I've kept things together well."

"Mom, I know you miss Dad. It's pretty obvious."

"Well," she resists the urge to scoot closer. "You've been a bright spot in my life—*the* bright spot in my life—these past two years."

"Well, there's your career."

"Yes. Well. You're more important." She stiffens. "And that's why I'm so serious when I talk to you about your fixation on this art thing. I know you're passionate about it, and that's wonderful, but I'm just trying to make sure you're looking out for your future."

There are only three more days of our trip together—three more days in Brussels, and then we go together to Ireland, where she drops me off at the program. If I can avoid one of the thousand fights we'll probably have between now and then, I'll be happy.

"Let's just figure out how we want to spend the rest of our time in Brussels," I say, and with a sigh that I accept as a resignation, my mom abandons the topic of my sad, terrible future as an unemployed art major.

"Why did Grandpa want you to spend this much time here?" my mom asks as she flips through the Rick Steves book on the bedside table.

"Actually, I booked the flights. I wasn't sure how long I'd want to stay. Belgium seemed exciting."

"Okay!" She says, trying to be a good sport. "So what's on your agenda for tomorrow?"

"Ummm, we could walk around some more? Get another waffle. Get some more fries. Oh! Check out the Tintin museum? Get another waffle after that?" It sounds excruciating. Honestly, the thought of one more day looking out at the dirty river and the plastic lawn chair hanging above it is enough to make me want to formally propose that they give Belgium back to France and the Netherlands. It's a terrible fake country, and it shouldn't exist.

"You never read Tintin books when you were younger, did you?" my mom asks.

I shake my head, and to my surprise she gives me a rare, honest-to-goodness, authentic Alice Parker smile.

"How about," my mom says, "we see if we can get an early flight to Ireland?" She pauses, waiting for my reaction.

"Oh, thank god," I say.

12

THE BUS CREAKS to a stop and opens its doors by the side of a road with no visible signs or street names. It suddenly occurs to me that the bus driver hasn't been announcing the names of stops, and even if he had been, I'm not sure I know exactly where we're supposed to get off. The same thought must occur to my mother, because she looks up from her book for the first time since we got on the bus.

"Which stop are we getting off at?" she asks.

"Um, trying to figure that out now."

She folds a corner of the page she's on and returns it to her bag. "Honestly, Nora, how were you going to do this without me?" She reaches into her bag and pulls out information from the Donegal Colony for Young Artists website.

The bus stops again, and a boy—an adorable boy, it should be noted—around my age gets on. He has dark curls and wears glasses that make him look like a model in a Warby Parker ad. He sits a few rows ahead of us and takes out a book, and I crane my neck to see what he's reading.

"Okay," my mom says. "It looks like we can either take the train to . . . no, we didn't do that . . . Oh, oh, we get off the number 2 bus at . . . do you think we've passed Ballyshannon already?"

"Why don't we ask someone on the bus to help us?" I say, looking at the boy.

"Ah! Nora. We got on the wrong bus. We needed to get on the 2. Look, this is the 5. We need to get off at the next stop and figure this out."

I don't have a better plan, and I don't argue. We make our way to the front of the bus, and I try to get a slightly better view of the boy's face, but I don't have time. The bus stops, and we get off, finding ourselves on a tiny strip with a bus station, a few houses, and what looks like a restaurant. We head toward the restaurant as I say a silent prayer for WiFi, and then, seeing how dark it looks inside the windows, an even more frantic silent prayer that it's open.

"You'd think the guidebook would have a FEW more specifics on public transportation," she mumbles, more to herself than to me. I'd seen the page on Donegal County (yes, just a page in an entire book about Ireland) and the two sentences that she'd underlined and highlighted: "Although the far-flung northern corner of Ireland doesn't have much in terms of high-profile attractions or museums, if you have a few extra days and a car, head up to enjoy the natural beauty of the coast and soak in some of the county's artistic history."

A sign on the restaurant's window indicates that they have WiFi. "Oh, thank the Great Leprechaun in the Sky," I say. And the place is open, though we seem to be the only people inside, and when we walk in, the waitress looks at us like we're the children of Bigfoot.

We sit and order two cups of coffee. "I'm going to ask the waitress," my mom says. The hair around her face has begun to frizz into a halo. It reminds me that I probably look like a shaved yeti. I've gone without makeup and hair products this entire trip so far, luckily because I've also gone more or less without mirrors. But now that I'm almost at the DCYA, I want to start looking somewhat presentable.

"So you didn't think to look up how to get to your camp in advance?" my mom asks. "What would you be doing right now if I weren't here?"

"I *did* look it up," I say. "I mean, I thought I did. And I'd be fine. Just like we're going to be fine." And then I remember the sign at the front of the restaurant.

"Hold on," I say. "As long as there's WiFi, let me get the e-mail for the contact person from the program and see if they can help." My mom might have shilled out the kidney the cell phone companies charge for overseas data on her own phone, but she definitely didn't for mine. Bet she regrets that now. I scroll through my e-mails and come to the one I remember. "Aha. Evelyn Wray. She's the woman we're staying with."

"Excuse me," my mother says to the waitress as she brings our coffee. "Which bus do we get on to get to Donegal?"

"Well, you're in County Donegal," she answers.

"No, well, yes. I mean the town Donegal?"

"Donegal *Town*," I add.

"Aye, well, you're not far. It's just down the N56, hop on the 5 bus right down the road here, and pop off a' the Diamond."

"We were on the right bus!" I say.

The waitress offers a sympathetic smile. "Tourists?"

"How can you tell?" I answer.

"Thank you. Very much," my mom says to the waitress, then puts some euros on the table. We go outside to take the next 5 bus that passes by, carefully sitting in the first row behind the driver. To my humiliation, my mother found it necessary to ask the bus driver every single stop whether we were in Donegal Town yet.

"You must be Nora." An older woman with brown shoulder-length hair approaches us right when we step off the bus.

"Hi, yes," I say. "Are you Evelyn?"

Instead of answering, she laughs and gives me a hug. "My husband and I have been hosting DCYA students for a decade now, and it's always so exciting to meet our newest guest! Come on, up with your suitcases."

"I'm Alice Parker." My mother extends her hand. "Thank you so much for letting me stay with you on such short notice."

"Not a problem at all, dear. Had the extra bedroom, as long as you don't mind a twin bed. And besides, it's quite exciting to have the family of Robert Parker here."

Evelyn loads both of our suitcases into the back of her car. Though she looks to be about sixty years old, she's surprisingly strong, and faster on her feet than either my mom or me. It might be the travel, or the flight, or the taking the wrong-but-actually-right bus to get here, but we are both fully zombified.

"DCYA is a great place," Evelyn says, looking in her rear-view mirror at me. "If Seamus—that's my husband, Seamus—and I had ever had kids, this is the type of program I wish they'd been admitted to. We've been friends with Declan and Áine for years now—they're the couple that runs the place, y'know. Brilliant folk. Áine is a professor at Trinity, over in Dublin, and Declan came from Cambridge."

My mother gives an approving murmur.

We're in the car for another twenty minutes, at least, Evelyn giving us a rundown on the local hangout spots and the shops that have gone in and out of business in the many years since she's lived in the north of Ireland.

"Here we are," she says finally, pulling off a windy road and down a dirt path. The front steps are littered with mis-matched galoshes. "You're going to want to borrow a pair of those if you head out to the farm—I'm sure Maeve or Callum will show you, Nora—if you want to visit the horses. Hello, horses!" She gives a little wave to a few *actual horses* in a barn deep in their backyard. I want to ask who Maeve and Callum are, but I'm too distracted by the actual, living, breathing live-stock in my vicinity.

"Are those . . . *your* horses?" my mom asks.

"Yeah, ah, but the little one's hurt 'is knee, poor thing. So no riding this time around, I'm afraid."

For a farmhouse on the rural coast of Ireland, the inside of Evelyn's home feels strangely familiar. We pass a washer and dryer, followed by a big kitchen table and living room. Two pictures hang side by side above the stove: a portrait of Pope John Paul II and one of John F. Kennedy.

We reach the stairs, and Evelyn ushers us up to the guest bedrooms.

"Now I know you're tired from your trip, but trust me, loves: I'm going to prepare a quick tea, you'll eat up, and then you'll go to the pub in town. I promise you'll have the best time."

"Tonight might not be the best night," my mom says. "We really are exhausted, and—"

"Pffft!" Evelyn interrupts with a burst of air and flap of her hand. "*Trust me.* Drop the bags, have a cuppa, and you'll be good as gold. A little *craic* never hurt."

"*Crack?*" My mother looks back and forth from me to Evelyn while the two of us exchange a glance.

"*Craic,*" Evelyn says again, slower, trying to emphasize the difference in spelling.

"*A-I-C,*" I say. "It's like Irish for 'fun.'"

"Oh, is Irish the language? I thought it was Gaelic?"

Evelyn answers quickly, "Yeah, one and the same. It's all Irish. Now set those bags down and come have some food!"

There are so many people in the pub that I wonder whether Donegal actually counts as the countryside at all—it seems like there are more people in here than there could possibly be in the entire town, in the whole county. For a pub called the Nook, it definitely feels more like a college bar than a sunny breakfast corner. It's all made of wood, like a tree house, almost vibrating with noise and swollen with the smell of beer and something a little sweet that I can't quite place.

"Drinking age in Ireland is eighteen, right?" I whisper to my mom as we weave our way through the bodies. I'm still seventeen. What are the odds that some burly Irish bouncer is going to card me and throw me out? I hold my bag closer to my chest while we slide past a group of middle-aged men in soccer jerseys drinking pints.

"I have no idea," she answers. "Is it eighteen? You shouldn't be going crazy tonight, right before your program starts."

"Okay," I say out of habit, and even though obviously it would have been all "part of the experience" or whatever to get wildly drunk at a pub in Ireland, it's not really something I need to do, especially because I'm not even much of a drinker at home, and it seems considerably less fun to do with my mom.

"I'll get us the drinks," my mom shouts over the blaring rock music.

"I'll grab a table!" I shout back, wriggling my way past a girl wearing a cheap veil and surrounded by friends with T-shirts that say: HEN PARTY. I find a wooden table with two chairs up against the far wall.

From my relatively quiet vantage point, I watch my mother. She's wearing gym shoes, yoga pants, and a black long-sleeved T-shirt, looking like she should be leaving an expensive spin class in New York City and absolutely under no circumstances drinking beer with strangers. It's like the scene from every Lifetime Original Movie where the hectic businesswoman who doesn't have time to appreciate the Christmas spirit somehow ends up at a homey family event, still wearing her power suit. You know, except for how for some reason all of Lifetime's movies hinge on the premise that Santa is real. My mom sticks out like a hangnail that you can't pull at because it just starts hurting more, and it's honestly kind of hilarious.

I instinctually pull out my sketchpad and begin drawing the outline of the scene in cartoon form: my mom, all angles in black, surrounded by a mound of rosy strangers.

"Hey," a voice next to me says. "You're drawing."

"Yeah," I say back. "I am indeed."

"In a pub."

"Yeah again." Once I finish shading my cartoon mom's left elbow, I turn to find the voice, and I see that I'm face-to-face with a mess of dark curls.

"You brought a book," I counter, pointing to the thick paperback sticking out of a satchel at his side.

"I have, yeah." He smiles and his entire face blushes, from his earlobes down his neck. He's wearing thick-rimmed glasses that cover most of his face, and even though it's quite warm in the bar, he's wearing a puffy red jacket.

"That's quite good!" he says, peeking over my shoulder. He pulls the opposite page from the one I'm working on toward him and flaps it up so he can see both sides. "These aren't half-bad."

I don't know whether I'm supposed to thank him or get angry at him for looking through my notebook without permission, so I do something halfway in between: "Thanks," I say, tugging the notebook away. It falls closed. I guess that's what I get for sketching in a bar like an antisocial lunatic.

"Hey, hey!" the boy says, pointing at the stickers on the front of my notebook. Lena bought them for me last year for my birthday; they're some of the characters I've drawn on Tumblr. She ordered an entire box, and I've been selling them from my website. Turns out, people like sticker versions of their favorite characters almost as much as they like personalized gay erotic scenes.

The stickers I have on my notebook are Bilbo and Legolas from *Lord of the Rings* taking a selfie (a commission), and the logo I drew for my site: Ophelia holding up the skull of Yorick instead of Hamlet, both she and the skull wearing sunglasses.

"*Lord of the Rings!*" he says

"Oh, yeah," I say. "Ha-ha."

"Do you like them? The books, I mean?" he asks, eager as a puppy dog.

"Actually, I haven't read them."

He takes a full step back and playfully slaps me on the arm. "Come on! My mates and I love those books. I forced them all to read them before eleventh year, and we stayed inside for a full summer term getting through the lot. I gotta say, though, I like those stickers better than the movies. What's that one?" he asks, pointing at the Ophelia sticker.

He talks in paragraphs. It's exhausting.

"Oh," I say, and then it slips out without my permission: "That's the logo for my blog, Ophelia in Paradise. I actually drew them—all the stickers, I mean—myself."

"Cool!" the boy says, and he grabs the notebook out of my hand to get a closer look. I should definitely be angry now—no one, not even Lena, is allowed to hold my notebook—but I don't mind. Is this how famous people feel every day? Do famous people get to feel special and interesting everywhere they go? How do I become a permanently famous person?

"I have more," I say, gently prying the notebook from his hands and opening it up to reveal the pages behind the front cover. "More commissions with *Lord of the Rings* characters, some from *Harry Potter* . . ." And then we hit one of Sherlock pressing John Watson up against the wall, John's face surprised beneath the kiss. "Oh, well, y'know," I say and shut the book quickly.

"Those are really decent! Mind if I take a picture for the mates? Send it out on the group chat? Hold on." He texts wildly for a few seconds, then flashes a picture of the stickers on my notebook. "A'ight. Solid. So you're here for the Deece, right?"

"What?" I say. "No, I mean, I don't—sorry, what?"

He laughs, and I love the sound of his laugh. It's a real one, higher in pitch than you'd expect, but just because it's actually full of joy, filtered through a mouth tightened into a smile.

"Sorry," he says. "The Deece. The DCYA. The art program."

Before I'm able to respond, I see Alice Parker—to my surprise, wielding two beers—standing over the boy's shoulder with a look like, "Who is this tall and semi-handsome Irish stranger that it looks as if you are suddenly on a date with?"

I give a shrug like, "I don't know, he just sat down and started texting, but he's kind of cute, right? And hey! He liked my art!" Or, at least, I convey *most* of that.

"My name is Callum, by the way," the boy says to me. He doesn't notice that my mom is standing right behind him.

"That's my mom," I respond.

"Oh," he says. "Hi, I'm Callum." He scrambles to his feet and extends a hand to her. She is holding two dripping glasses, so she can't shake back. He realizes this and withdraws his hand. "Right," he says. "I'm just going to pop over to the bar." And he slides off.

"Who was that?" My mom raises her eyebrows.

"I don't know. He just sat down. But he liked my art! I mean, not my real art, just the online stuff."

"Your *stuff* is online?"

Shit. How can I backtrack? "No, the stuff I draw of things online, some of my drawings. He just knew the characters from the front of my notebook. On Tumblr." My answer is so nonsensical that my only hope is that she'll assume she doesn't understand it because she doesn't know how the Internet works. "You know, Instagram," I add confidently, trying to confuse her as much as possible.

It works.

"He was cute," my mom says. Hearing your mom talk about boys she thinks are cute is the stuff they should have warned us about in cheesy videos in health class.

"Sort of," I say. I don't add "if you like a sexy librarian who played in an emo band in high school and is embarrassed about it but still has better taste in music and books than anyone he knows. You've got to like that sort of thing."

I take a far bigger sip of the dark beer in front of me than I should. The last time I had a beer was the night Nick took me to his basement, which is not a memory I'm looking to relive. Even though I'm across an entire ocean, in a tiny Irish pub— basically as far physically and thematically from the suburbs of Chicago as it gets, really—I still just think of Nick and it causes my insides to shrivel up. I suddenly get the urge to go on Facebook and see the selfie that Lena posted of the two of them lying side by side on her couch. It's a masochistic urge. Twist a knife in my own stomach, why don't I.

This beer doesn't taste anything like that one. That beer was thin and watery, with a tang left from the can it came from. This one is dark and malty. It tastes a little bit like cinnamon and coffee.

"You should go talk to him!" my mother says.

"Who?"

"The boy who was here."

And so in this distinctly *Twilight Zone* episode of my life, where my mom is with me, drinking in a pub in the Irish countryside, where a boy I've never met before wants to talk to me and likes my drawings, I put my notebook away and go and find the cute stranger to talk to him again.

13

"SO, WHAT BOOK is that?" I ask, finally managing to elbow my way past a half dozen semi-intoxicated Irishmen and squeeze in next to Callum. "I mean, the one in your bag."

He smiles at me, revealing incisors that are slightly too long, like a vampire or a teen wolf. For whatever reason, I find it ridiculously sexy.

"It's dumb," he says. "Silly, I mean." He pulls out a paperback copy of *The Silmarillion* so tattered and weather-worn, it looks like it crossed the ocean on a life raft to make its way to Callum.

"So, are you really a big *Lord of the Rings* fan?" I ask.

"Oh yeah. You at least seen the films?

"Yeah, I've seen them," I lie. By "seen them," I mean I saw a few minutes of the first one when it was on TV and then turned it off because the old hobbit made a really, really scary face and it was far too late for me to have to deal with that when

I closed my eyes that night. I can barely wrap my mind around real history, let alone the entire medieval history of a magical kingdom. I do like Orlando Bloom with blond hair, though.

"So, *are* you here for the Deece?"

"Yeah," I answer. "The Deece." I like the sound of it in my mouth. "You too?"

Callum laughs and puts one of his hands on my shoulder as if to steady himself. "Jesus, no. I mean, I'm actually there plenty because I've known Áine and Declan forever, but you should see me try to draw. Nothing like your stuff. I dropped out around stick figures."

"You live here?" I ask. I'm finding it difficult to wrap my head around the notion that someone could live his entire life in a small town in a corner of an island so far away from everything.

"Well, sort of, yeah. My mum's in Dublin—I go to school out there, but I spend the summers with my da' and uncles here."

"I can't believe you thought your friends would like my drawings," I say. *Prevent these words from coming out of your mouth, Nora! You don't want him to think you're an insane, self-centered American, which, yes, okay, you might be, but let's go as long as possible without him figuring that out, shall we?*

"Ha, I mean, they're really good! You totally capture the characters. Like something they should put on BuzzFeed or something."

"Wait, you have BuzzFeed here?"

"Ha! This is Ireland, not, like, Soviet-era Ukraine. They have BuzzFeed everywhere. I remember a mate of mine from last summer—she was also from America—was shocked that I watched *Breaking Bad*. Like, she didn't realize we have Netflix."

I try to focus on Callum's words, but suddenly, a voice in my head starts nagging me: *He's been at the Deece every year since he was little. He's seen American girls come and go. You're no different.*

I push the voice away.

"What about you?" Callum asks. "Where you from? And . . . oh, what's your name? Lord, did I really go this long without asking your name?"

"It's Nora. Nora Parker-Holmes, like with a hyphen. And I'm from Chicago."

"All right, Nora Parker-Holmes-like-with-a-hyphen from Chicago, what's your . . . least favorite film?"

"My least favorite film?"

"Come on, isn't that a more interesting question than 'What's your favorite film?'" The stool beside Callum is vacated, and he taps it, inviting me up to sit next to him. "You want a drink?"

"No, I'm good, thanks." *Does he think I'm a loser because I'm not drinking?* "And . . . um . . . my least favorite movie is *Donnie Darko*."

"What? Noooo! I love that film!" Callum turns his body around to face me, so intent on having this discussion that his eyes lock in on mine. And then he places both of his hands on my shoulders, sending tingles down my spine. "Wait," he says. "Hold on. We are going to have this proper showdown, but first tell me all the boring stuff: age, hometown, hopes and dreams, you know."

"I'm Chicago born and raised . . . sort of. I'm actually from the area just outside Chicago. And . . . my grandpa is an artist, and he paid for me to come to Europe. And . . . my mom decided to tag along." I realize as I'm saying it how absolutely, horrifically boring my life is. There are teenagers in the world who sail across oceans alone, or who grow up as child soldiers, or who cure measles in their backyard using chemicals they find in fertilizer. And here I am, doodling on a notepad and dyeing some of my hair green and pretending it makes me special.

"And you have shite taste in films," Callum adds.

"I beg to differ. And what's your least favorite movie?" I say.

"*Avengers: Age of Ultron.* Not empirically, but just such a letdown coming from Joss. Like, it was a fine film, but I wanted so much better after *Winter Soldier* was so good, you know?"

Whichever angel in heaven sent me a hot boy with an Irish accent who likes the Avengers as much as I do, thank you. I will sing hymns in your honor. I will write hymns in your honor. If you are an Irish angel, I will spell it "honour" in order to properly honour you.

Callum inverts his glass and lets the few remaining drops fall onto his tongue. "Can I ask you something else?" he says, and before I give an answer, he asks. "Why is your blog called Ophelia in Paradise?"

I smile. "I don't really know, to be honest. We read *Hamlet* in English class, and I really liked it. It was the first Shakespeare play I actually, you know, understood, kind of? The idea of this boy coming back from college and having everything in his life be different, and being faced with having to do the right thing when there's no one telling you what the right thing is? And not having parents around with the 'right answer' the way they were when you were a kid, you know? Because his mom is part of the problem, and he and we don't know if his dad is actually real or if it's just the manifestation of his guilt.

"And he comes up with just the worst plans—he pretends to be crazy, he puts on this whole play, he escapes from pirates . . . I don't know. I feel bad for him. I had this vision of him on a beach somewhere, just drinking a piña colada and reading a book and not having to worry about the state of Denmark or his soul."

"So how come Ophelia then?" he says.

I take a breath. The truth is I made the blog last year when Nick and I were . . . if not dating, then that horrifically non-descript nonsense, a "thing." When I didn't tell Lena about it because I was embarrassed. Because I knew it wouldn't last. Because, the little voice inside reminded me, I always knew, on some level, that he was using me.

I had waited in the driveway that night for Nick to pick me up in his Jeep. I lied to my mom, saying I was getting picked up by a girl from my chem class to work on a presentation together. When I got in the car, he and I exchanged an awkward greeting.

"Hi."

"Hey."

We didn't hug or kiss. We drove in silence. I had read in *Seventeen* that one of the most sensitive parts of a boy's body was the hair where his head meets his neck, because it's so rarely touched, so while Nick DiBasilio drove, I ran my left hand along the back of his prickly-soft crew cut. He didn't say anything, but he didn't tell me to stop, so I kept it up while he turned off the highway, past downtown, and toward the beach.

The beach is closed at night, but we didn't go there to go to the beach. He pulled into a parking spot and turned off the engine. I withdrew my hand from his neck, and it hovered between us until, with a wave of confidence, I placed it on his jeans. Even through the fabric I could feel he was hard.

The next day I texted him: *What's up?*

He responded an hour later: *Not too much.*

Nothing else. No details about his day, not even a half-hearted: *U?*

In that moment, I understood Ophelia more than I had in half a semester of my English teacher's lectures. Whether the boy you love is mad or pretending to be mad, wanting someone you can't understand or who won't let you understand will make you go mad yourself. Waiting for his affection was a version of Chinese water torture, desperately waiting for the next drop of any sign that he might like me, unsure when it would come, if it came at all.

"I don't know," I tell Callum. "I just think she deserves more credit."

Callum readjusts in his seat and clears his throat. He checks his phone, smiles a little to himself, then quickly turns his attention back to me. "I never actually read *Hamlet*, to be totally honest," he says. "We were supposed to, I think."

Now I blush. He probably thinks I'm insane. I just went on

a rant about Shakespeare. In a bar. And I don't even know his last name. "What's your last name?" I ask.

"Cassidy," he says.

"Callum Cassidy. No wonder you like superheroes."

"What do you mean?"

"Callum Cassidy—CC. You know, like Lex Luthor, Lois Lane, Jessica Jones, Bucky Barnes, Bruce Banner, Pepper Potts . . . You're practically a superhero yourself."

"You know a lot of comic book characters off the top of your head."

"I read a lot of comics when I was younger. And I have a good memory," I say.

"Well, there's no telling with me—I might turn out to be a super villain, like . . . Doctor Doom, DD."

"What would your superpower be?"

"I would destroy my opponent with my knowledge of obscure *Lord of the Rings* trivia. What would yours be?"

I think for a minute. "I would . . . be able to draw anything and make it come to life."

Callum pounds a fist on the table in mock anger. "That one is so much better than mine! I shouldn't have gone first! By the way, I like your . . ." He gestures to the green streak in my hair.

"Thanks," I twirl it absentmindedly. "My mom hates it."

Callum Cassidy doesn't respond, and he breaks eye contact for the first time in fifteen minutes to look over my shoulder.

"Nora, honey." It's my mom. And she's right behind me. Luckily I'm almost positive she didn't hear me say she hated my streak, or else she almost certainly would not have called me "honey."

"It's getting late," she says. "We've had a long day. I'm tired. I think it's time to head back."

Right on cue. Just when, for the first time in my life, a cute boy seems actually interested in having a conversation with me. Now I remember exactly why I wanted to travel by myself in the first place—because when I'm alone, I get to choose where and when I go, and I don't have to be responsible for anyone else or how they're feeling or how they may or may not be tired just as I'm getting to know the coolest guy I've met in a really long time.

But, as I remind myself, she's leaving in a few days. And then I'll have the rest of my time in Ireland AND my entire trip to London and Florence to be on my own and have conversations with hot guys for as long as I want.

I shoot Callum an apologetic look.

"Can I get your number or something?" he asks.

My mother is watching us both, holding her coat over her arm. "Um," I say, "I'm not sure my phone does the whole international texting thing, but Facebook? Here, let me see your phone." He hands it over, and I open the Facebook app. I type in my name and request to be friends with myself. "There," I say.

"Let's hang out later this week or something," Callum says. "I didn't get a chance to knock some sense into you about *Donnie Darko*, cinematic masterpiece."

"Sure," I say. "Sounds fun."

"Hey, wait!" he calls just as I'm leaving. "Take this." He shoves his copy of *The Silmarillion* into my hands. "I've read it a hundred times. I consider it a public service to spread the gospel."

"Okay," I say. "Thank you."

He just smiles, and I smile back, and then I follow Alice Parker outside the pub. My ears ring in the sudden quiet.

"Did you have fun?" she says.

"I don't know," I say. "I guess." Teenage angst is a hard habit to break.

"Well, I had a good time," she says.

I run my fingers across the soft pages of the book Callum gave me. "Yeah," I say. "I did too."

14

"**I SPENT TWENTY** years learning to paint like Raphael and a life-time learning to paint like a child."

Declan pauses for effect. "Those immortal words, spoken by . . ." He pauses again and gestures with a sweep of his hand out to the classroom.

"Picasso," the entire class minus me chants in unison.

"Picasso," I say, half a beat too late.

"Yes, Pablo Picasso. Good old Pablo. That shall be the credo for this course over the next three weeks. Yes, art is subjective. But whether you're impressionists, cubists, dadaists, what have you, here at the Deece, we'll be studying the fundamentals."

"While still fostering your own artistic vision," Áine interrupts.

We're just two hours into the program, and I already get their dynamic: a classic good cop, bad cop routine. I wouldn't have actually believed they were married if they hadn't told us.

Declan is about six foot five, bald, with a dark beard that he strokes incessantly, twirling his fingers through his mustache like a cartoon villain. He wears a full suit with a polka-dot tie and matching socks.

Áine, meanwhile, is about a foot and a half shorter than Declan, with a pixie cut and a pixie nose and an affability and choice of clothing that gives off the general vibe of *pixie*.

"We've been running this program for fifteen years," Áine chirps (chirping thus far seems to be her primary mode of communication), "and we've seen artists at all levels, all styles, and all natural abilities. The important thing is that you each find and follow your own artistic path."

We're in Studio B, which implies that there are probably more studios, although I didn't see any on the shortcut Evelyn pointed out through her backyard to get here. According to universal high school lore (aka something every single person claims happened at *their* high school), a gaggle of intrepid seniors got their hands on two greased pigs and released them into the school, labeled #1 and #3 so that the administration spent all day looking for the missing, nonexistent pig #2. From what I've seen so far, it doesn't seem out of the realm of possibility that there's only one studio labeled *B* as a joke.

The room looks more like a museum than a studio: glass-fronted bookshelves filled with skulls and taxidermied animals line the walls. One entire wall is devoted to a framed display of delicately pinned butterflies. A skeleton that I'm almost positive is real slouches in the corner, wearing a top hat and tie with the Union Jack.

As for the students, there are eight of us: six girls and two boys. The only other American is a boy from California whose name and face are equally forgettable, like a contestant on *The Bachelorette* who'd get eliminated on week two. He definitely introduced himself, but once he turned away, I couldn't have picked him out of a two-man police lineup if catching the Zodiac Killer was on the line.

POLICE: All right, Nora, one of these men is the Zodiac Killer, notorious San Francisco terror, and the other is a teenager from California in your program whom you met only moments ago. Please tell us which is which.

ME: Can I have a hint?

It seems that a few of the students are from Dublin and already know one another, some are from England, and one of the girls, a lanky blonde with a laugh I can hear from across the room, is from Australia. There's only one girl actually from Donegal; her name is Maeve.

"So now," Declan says, clapping his hands together and then fixing his cufflinks, "partner up, and we'll start our first activity."

It's like gym class all over again. Why do teachers think teens ever enjoy partnering up, let alone on their first day, when they don't know anyone? What happened to *don't judge a book by its cover* and all that? How else are we supposed to judge when we're forced to pick partners on our very first day?

I turn to the boy next to me, one of the Brits, and try to make eye contact, but he's clearly already partnered up with California-maybe-Zodiac-Killer.

From across the room, a pair of eyes latch onto mine. "Pair up?" says my angel. It's Maeve.

"For sure."

Áine rings a bell to get our attention. "For our first class, we're going to get to know one another a bit. First, face your partner."

Maeve and I square our stools and look at each other. She gives me a small smile and then winks. She's so much calmer than I am.

"Open to a blank page in your notebook, and pick up your pencil. You're going to draw your partner's face."

"BUT," Declan adds with an air of mischief that seems to delight him a little too much, "you're not allowed to look at your page. You're to maintain eye contact with your partner the entire time. You have ten minutes. GO!"

And suddenly there's a scramble of paper and squeaking chairs. Áine sashays to the stereo in the corner and begins playing metal music with a thumping bassline.

I flip to a clean page, take a deep breath, and look up at Maeve's face, into her eyes that stare right back into mine.

The exercise is so much harder than it sounds. Right away, I fight the urge to glance down at my paper. Maeve still seems impossibly relaxed, half-smiling while looking right at my face like this is perfectly normal for her.

"So, where are you from?" she asks, her hand still moving impossibly fast across the page. "America, yeah?"

"Yeah," I reply, finding it difficult to multitask.

"But, like, New York? L.A.?"

"Actually, the suburbs of Chicago." I don't mean to sound so abrupt, but I'm desperately trying to draw something not terrible. All of my concentration is on making sure my drawing doesn't end up looking like Mrs. Potato Head. "And . . . you . . . are from here?"

"Yup!" she replies, and from the corner of my eye I can tell that she's shading. *How is she shading? How does she know where to shade?* "Our place is actually right up the road from the studio."

"Oh, your parents live around here? That's nice." Turns out, when I'm concentrating, my conversational skills fall somewhere between uninterested waitress and lobotomized zombie.

Maeve gives a little laugh. "Because I don't spend enough time with them."

As if on cue, Áine comes up behind her and glances down at her page. "Try to lengthen your lines," Áine says to Maeve. Maeve nods, never lifting her eyes from my face. When Áine looks down at my work, she gives a cursory nod and small smile. I'm left feeling half-proud that my work was satisfactory and half-disappointed that I didn't get more attention.

Time passes, but I'm staring so deeply into Maeve's blue eyes that I can't tell if it's been five minutes or forty minutes.

"And . . . time!" Declan bellows, as everyone but me drops

their pencil immediately. I drop mine half a beat late. This seems to be a trend.

"And now the fun part. Everyone, bring me your drawings, and we're going to play a little guessing game."

For the first time since the page was blank, I look down. My drawing is an absolute mess—lopsided features and ears that look like cartoon snails. Stomach burning with shame, I trudge up to Declan and hand him my drawing.

"And now we mix them up," Declan says, shuffling the papers. He then posts them on the wall. "Try to find your-selves! Off you pop!"

Mine is easy. I instantly recognize my face because Maeve is a wizard who either cheated or has the ability to see through her hands like a blind fairytale character. She somehow man-aged to put together a series of lines that actually look like my face. She captured an essence about me, an impatience in my expression that makes me look alert and thoughtful. I'd be jeal-ous if I weren't so impressed.

Luckily, with the exception of Maeve, it doesn't look like anyone else's drawing is that much better than mine. "Circle up," Áine says. "Let's check portraits and introduce ourselves properly."

There are a few mismatched portraits, which inspires laugh-ter and the exchange of drawings. When it's my turn, I decide to keep my introduction short and sweet: "Hi, I'm Nora. I'm going to be a senior in high school, and I'm from the suburbs of Chicago. In America." Boring, maybe, but I'm on the spot. It doesn't matter what I say anyway, because everyone's attention turns immediately to Maeve's drawing of me.

"Woah," someone says. "It actually looks just like her!"

"Who drew that one?"

"Uh, Maeve," I say.

Maeve smiles sweetly and looks down. When she's up, nobody comments on the drawing I did. We get to keep each other's drawings of us, but I wish I could have mine back. I'm overcome with the urge just to rip it up into as many pieces as physically possible.

A gray cat the color of lint and larger than any cat should be weaves between my legs and starts making a noise that's less purring and more vibrating. Áine dips in and picks the cat up, causing it to immediately droop in her arms like it's given up on being a sentient being.

"Maeve, will you make sure Bartholomeow behaves?" she says, shoving the cat onto Maeve's lap. Already, Maeve is the favorite. She had the best drawing, and Áine already trusts her with the studio cat. Once Bartholomeow is on Maeve's lap, he begins purring. In fact, I think he might actually be snoring. Oh great, she's a cat whisperer too. Gold stars for Maeve, insecurity complexes for the rest of us.

15

Dear Lena,

So I'm two days into the program, and it's insanely cool/intimidating/fun/inspiring/terrifying. When I say we're in rural Ireland, this is what you should picture: a small town, and then twenty minutes away from the small town, a road with a pub and a church. And then, surrounded by farmland, the studio where we work. When you get to town, it's a different story, but I swear, there are more cows and sheep than people in the one-mile radius around my studio.

The program is run by this married couple: Declan and Áine (which I have yet to pronounce correctly—it's harder than it seems). Declan dresses like the headmaster of the world's most fashionable prep school—he's always in a full suit with a jacket and tie, and most of them are patterned. I can't describe how odd it is to see a man in a polka-dot suit and purple shoes strolling through a field filled with dirty farm equipment and horses too old to ride. It's like an *Alice in Wonderland* fever dream. He's definitely the hard-ass of the program. In two days he's given us about half a dozen lectures on technique and muscle memory and forgetting anything about your work that you considered to be any good and starting over from the ground up.

Áine (even in my head I know I'm pronouncing it wrong; maybe you can do better than me) is like everyone's mom here. I've never heard her say anything critical of anyone's work. Like, the worst that she's said was yesterday, when one of the boys (he's from California, but I can't remember his name) was painting a landscape from the window, and the colors were totally off. Áine suggested that he try painting the rest of it without touching white or black paint. And so he really had to focus on the colors of things—that fence isn't really black, it's dark blue with green streaks, you know. <u>And it came out so much better!</u> Áine is all about "releasing your inner artist" (she says that all the time). Everyone loves her.

My real mother, on the other hand, has been fine, considering. Still clearly missing my dad and worried about her job, for some reason, even though she said that taking a vacation wouldn't be an issue at all. I do feel bad. She's lonely, and she's been lonely since she and dad got divorced.

I think I told you about the time I came downstairs around eleven P.M. and saw her watching their wedding video. I was behind the couch, so I couldn't actually see her face, just her reflection in the window. And she was crying. I didn't know what to do. I guess, now, in retrospect, I should have comforted her, told her that it was for the best, that I love her, and that I'm here for her, but in retrospect everything's easy. I was embarrassed for her. I snuck back upstairs as quietly as I could and managed to get back into bed without her hearing me.

Is there a long German word that sums up the combination of shame and discomfort when a child sees her parent cry? It's this terrible combination of wanting to help someone you love but hating the feeling that you have to be the one to comfort your parent. Is this making any sense? I'm sorry I'm rambling. The good news is, she's leaving in two days, and so I won't have to worry about this anymore or be distracted from my art.

My art! The art here is really hard, and everyone is really, really good. We sketched this animal skull that Declan placed in the middle of the table. You would have hated it. Just imagine three hours of near silence (just the low background jazz music Declan plays) while we all just drew in a circle. Mine came out fine, a little lopsided, but fine. But almost everyone else's had . . . something. I don't know. Being here for two days around real artists, other people who take their art seriously—it makes me nervous.

Maybe I'm not as good as I thought I was. I mean, I'm fine. I can draw, I know I can. But, like, one of the girls, Maeve, draws things that I could pick out as hers anywhere on the planet. She has something special. Maybe that's the kind of thing you need to make it as an artist. Oh, and Maeve is also Declan and Áine's actual daughter! She lives here, near Donegal, with the coolest parents in the world, probably making art together all the time. I am almost positive the universe will reach its heat death before I make art with my mother. And of course she's gorgeous, with thick black hair and bangs like Zooey Deschanel, and she's skinny in a way that everything she wears looks good on her. And the worst part is I can't hate her because she's also insanely nice. People like that are the worst.

I did meet a boy—insert blushing emoji here, ha-ha— named Callum Cassidy, and yes, he is real, and yes, he is as adorably Irish as he sounds. We met at a pub my first night here (ALICE WAS ALSO AT THE PUB. IT WAS AS STRANGE AS IT SOUNDS), and he promised that we'd hang out again soon, even though it's been a full thirty hours and he hasn't messaged me yet. I hope Nick is better at texting you. The trip to Six Flags looked fun from your Instagrams.

So, here's hoping that the next two and a half weeks actually turn me into a good enough artist to get into RISD. Maeve could probably get in with both hands tied behind her back, painting with a brush in her mouth.

> Love you, miss you,
> hugs and kisses
> and all that,
> Nora

"I think it's cute that you and Lena are writing each other real letters, with pen and paper," my mom says as she slinks into my room. "I didn't think any of you kids still did that."

I'm not sure if she's trying to be friendly or passive-aggressive. It's so hard to tell with her sometimes. "Well, Grandpa gave me that beautiful stationery."

"And it's nice that you're putting it to good use." She sits on the corner of my bed. It's the same pose she was in on my bed back home when she told me she and my dad were getting a divorce. She must realize it, because she almost immediately stands back up and runs her hand over the comforter to smooth out its wrinkles. "Is everything okay with you and Lena, with her new boyfriend? I know that can be hard sometimes."

What is this conversation? Why does my mom think that just by coming into my room, we'll suddenly have a magical *Gilmore Girls* relationship where we dish and gab about how my best friend just starting dating the boy who took my virginity then stopped talking to me, and how that same best friend still doesn't know. Because I didn't tell her. Because I was embarrassed. Because I was heartbroken.

"It's totally fine," I say. "We're fine. Why wouldn't we be?"

In a completely un-Alice move, my mom ignores the sharpness in my voice.

"How was the first day of your program?" she asks.

What I could say: Well, to be honest, it was kind of stressful because all the other kids have cool accents and seem so sophisticated. They already have unique artistic voices, and I'm just here trying to go from cartoons to serious art and realizing that everything I've been taught just isn't enough. And what if you were right all along? Being a professional artist is hard, but I was always willing to put the work in. But it's becoming increasingly obvious that my talents are above average at best, so what if hard work isn't enough?

What I do say: It was fine!

149

I see by the look on her face that this was the wrong answer. "Fine?" she repeats back. "I come in here asking about your day, about the program that we both traveled halfway around the world to get to, and you give me 'fine'?"

"I never asked you to come, okay? I've made that abundantly clear."

"Well, I *am* here, and I asked my daughter how her day went."

"It was kind of stressful, okay? I'm used to drawing cartoons. I don't do a lot of this stuff, and a lot of the other students are really good at it."

She needs to take a moment to process the realization that I actually confided something about my life. "Maybe it's a good wake-up call, that art makes a better hobby."

The fury in my chest that I had been letting carefully dim erupts. This is why I didn't share with her in the first place.

"Mom. I don't want your advice right now," I say as calmly as I can. If I start yelling, the argument is lost. "I have a friend who gives me advice." I gesture to the letter I'm sending to Lena. "And I need to be around people who actually *respect* what I'm doing and how hard it is."

My mom opens her mouth, and in that split second I'm not sure if it's going to be rage or apology, and maybe neither is she, because just then the door opens and Evelyn pops her head through the gap.

"Sorry to interrupt, darlings. Alice, dear, can I get your help downstairs?"

The timing is too perfect. I wonder if Evelyn had been waiting outside the door, hearing our conversation grow more tense, waiting for the best moment to pull my mom away before we exploded like a cigarette and a gas station.

My mom nods and follows Evelyn out.

Two more days. Just two more days and my mother will be on a plane back to Chicago.

16

I FEEL LIKE I'm in one of Grandpa's paintings. My mom, Evelyn, and I sit by the fireplace (with an actual fire going, I might add) and quietly read while rain patters against the window. Evelyn insisted on pouring each of us a glass of Baileys ("Over ice! The only way to drink it!"), and so now here I am: in an armchair, a book in my left hand and a glass of dessert-flavored alcohol in my right hand, like I'm a retired shipping magnate at his seaside manor, waiting for his trained beagle to bring him slippers.

My mom has been devouring a copy of *Pride and Prejudice* that Evelyn had in her library, reading feverishly, as if Elizabeth Bennett and Mr. Darcy were flirting and fighting in real time. I see the appeal: Minus the whole "needing her daughter to get married as soon as possible," my mother is Mrs. Bennett incarnate, incapable of keeping herself out of every detail of my life.

"Find any characters in there that you relate to particularly well?" I ask.

"I'm reading, honey," she says. And she goes back to the book.

I sigh. And then I sigh again, a little bit louder, because no one seemed to recognize or care about the original sigh. I'm bored, that's the problem. I've spent so much time painting and drawing in the studio that if I pull out my sketchpad, I think my hands will take over for my brain and start drawing the words: PLEASE STOP GIVE US A BREAK. I sigh a third time, even louder, but neither Evelyn nor my mother responds. I bounce up and down on the chair a little bit, kicking my legs.

"Mind the cushions," Evelyn says, her eyes never leaving her book.

I turn to the window and pick a single droplet of water to trace as it floats down the pane. It's like a horse race. I root for my droplet to win, silently willing it to combine with nearby droplets to gain mass and speed. *There! Go!* It's almost made it to the window ledge and—

"Nora. Stop shaking your leg." My mother's voice distracts me from the water droplet, and I miss its moment of landing.

"I feel like I'm a sixty-five-year-old retired shipping magnate in his seaside manor, waiting for, like, trained beagles to bring me my slippers."

No one responds to my hilarious joke.

I sigh again, even louder, and try to go back to my book. It was written by a semi-famous white boy, and it contains humorous short stories that were published in the *New Yorker* that everyone called wry and deft. For some reason, I haven't been able to get through the first story (about a fisherman who's trying to catch boots on purpose).

I'm saved by a glorious ding from my cell phone. (If Pavlov were still alive, he'd have a hell of a time watching teenagers salivate at the sound of an iPhone notification.) My heart practically leaps out of my chest when I see that I've just received a Facebook message from Irish superhero Callum Cassidy.

Callum Cassidy: up to much?

Nora Parker-Holmes: nah. just at home (evelyn's home), reading and drinking baileys

Callum Cassidy: Sounds like Grandpa's ideal evening.

I am vindicated!

Nora Parker-Holmes: hahahahahahahahahaha

Callum Cassidy: new plan: come out with me and some mates to a cèilidh in town

Problem: It's still raining outside, and it's about a twenty-minute walk to town. There's no way I can get there without looking like a drowned rat. Follow up concern: This is a random boy I met in a bar. Aren't young women warned about that? After all, there is a distinct and altogether completely legitimate possibility that I was so distracted by Callum's accent that I missed signs of him being a complete creep.

<u>Completely Plausible Scenario</u>

IRISH-ACCENTED BOY
I enjoy hobbies such as staring at the sun
and kicking babies.
ME
(Distracted by said accent)
Please let me put my face on your face.

On the other hand, he likes to read. And he liked my cartoons. And has that accent. And hey! I'm young! And I want to go to a party with a cute Irish boy whose name I can't pronounce.

There's still, of course, the rain issue.

Callum Cassidy: I can come pick u up in 20

That was easy.

Nora Parker-Holmes: I'm in! See you soon :)

I contemplate the use of a winky face but decide it's best to leave something to the imagination.

"I'm going to a party!" I announce to the room.

Evelyn smiles.

"With whom?" my mother says.

"Uh, that boy I met at the pub. And some of his friends."

Alice closes *Pride and Prejudice*, which is how I know she's serious, because there was not a single point in the past hour when she has lifted her eyes from the page. "You're running off with a boy when you don't even know his name? Or where he's from?"

"I do know his name!" What a great feeling. It's like when the teacher calls on you because she doesn't think you're paying attention, and truth be told you're not, but then you get the answer right anyway. "It's Callum. Callum Cassidy! And he lives with his mom in Dublin!"

My mom pauses. "And where is this party?"

"I don't know exactly, but he said he'd pick me up." I hear it as I say it, the assertion that it's totally fine to get in a car headed toward an unknown place with a strange boy in a foreign country where I know no one. It screams *red flag*.

My mom's mouth tightens into a thin line. "I'm worried about you. I know you want to have a good time with your friends, and I want that for you too, but this is a worrisome situation."

I can't really defend the choice, other than by resorting to a petulant tantrum, which statistically and historically has a very low success rate, but before I can even stop myself the words spill out: "*This* is exactly why everything would be better if you weren't here."

I can see I've hurt her. She recoils at the words and folds her hands on her lap tightly. "I'm sorry," I murmur, and I'm not sure if she hears me or not, because she doesn't react.

And then my guardian angel makes another appearance.

"Callum is a sweet boy," Evelyn says, putting her book down on her lap and clasping her hands together.

"You know him?" My mother's face softens just a bit.

"Of course," Evelyn says. "The Cassidys live just up the road. Callum's a good boy. I've known him since he was a tyke. Nora will be fine!"

My mom turns back to look at me, and I give her my most responsible smile.

"Okay," she says. "Try to be back before midnight?" She looks back at Evelyn, who nods, and I breathe a giant sigh of relief. *I'm going to a party with a cute Irish boy named Callum!*

I look down at the flannels and oversized Northwestern hoodie that I'm wearing. "I'm going to change." Evelyn smiles, and my mom, in pure Mrs. Bennett fashion, nods enthusiastically. And I smile in spite of myself, thinking of my mom reading in Evelyn's chintz chair and wanting me to have a good time.

Callum arrives in a green pickup truck, because my life has suddenly become a Taylor Swift song. EDM that I don't recognize blasts from the speakers, and an iPhone attached to an aux cord dangles precariously from the dashboard. A boy is already in the front seat, so I slide into the back.

"Nora, Michael. Michael, Nora." Callum needs to shout so that we can hear him over the music. "Should've made him slide in back for you. Michael's not much of a gentleman."

"It's okay," I shout back. "I'm not that insulted."

Michael gives a loud fake sigh. "Nope. Nope. I'm afraid this won't do." With the car still moving, Michael unbuckles his seatbelt and wriggles his way into the backseat, where he plops next to me. "It's all yours."

Callum rolls his eyes in the rearview mirror.

"I'm not sure I can climb through without getting your seats muddy," I say, slightly more concerned about my ability to make a graceful landing without showing Callum my bare ass than the cleanliness of his car.

Callum laughs. "They've seen worse than your shoes. Remind me to tell you about the time I drove Michael back from Galway. We rescued a baby cow. The backseat smelled like manure for months." He pats the seat next to him, inviting me up.

"Don't look at my butt," I say, glancing over my shoulder toward Michael. He gamely covers his eyes, and, though I narrowly miss elbowing Callum in the jaw, I manage to make it into the passenger seat, dignity intact.

We drive for a few minutes across darkened roads before I finally ask the question: "So . . . what is a cèilidh?" I pronounce it "seel-duh." I can sense both boys smiling in the semi-dark.

"You want to take this one?" Michael asks.

"So," Callum says, taking his eyes off the road briefly to look at me, then looking back at the road, then looking back at me. "First, it's pronounced like 'kay-lee.'"

"Irish spelling is totally fucked," Michael calls from the backseat. "I apologize on behalf of the nation."

Callum clears his throat. "As I was saying, it's basically a party. But, like, a traditional party. Or—sorry—not traditional, but, like, kids dancing to Celtic music and just all of us getting together, you know? Dancing together."

"If Callum could ever get a girl to dance with him," Michael says.

Callum's eyes go wide, and he reaches back to try to hit his friend in the backseat.

"I kid, I kid!" Michael calls. "Uncle!"

Callum withdraws his arm.

"Besides," Michael says slyly, "we all know the real issue is our mate having a few too many girls to dance with, if you know what I mean."

"Shut it!" Callum says.

But we're all smiling. The car is so warm I feel drunk already.

We finally arrive, and I notice a microphone is set up in the corner on a makeshift wooden stage. I wonder if someone will be performing later.

"C'mon," Michael says. "Let's get you a drink!"

"Got it!" Callum says and disappears into the flow of dancing teens to get us some alcohol. I was worried before I left that I'd be out of place in my jeans and tank top (I traveled light and neglected the possibility that a cute boy would invite me to a party), but now that I'm here, it's apparent that I could have worn my flannels and been fine. People's outfits are all over the map—some girls are in dresses, while others, like me, are in jeans and boots. Everyone is wet and slightly muddy from the rain, and they're all perfectly okay with it.

Callum returns with two bottles of beer. He clinks his bottle against mine, takes a sip, and then says, "Come on, let's dance."

So I do. I don't know any of the steps, but I stare down at my feet with enough focus that I manage not to stomp on anyone else's feet. The dance moves seem to be: step, kick, kick, kick, then a swing—where Callum wraps his arm around my arm and spins me around as fast as we can go.

After dancing for a while, I tell Callum that I'm going to grab some water, and I head to the bar. I'm just leaving when I see Maeve a few stools down.

"Hi!" I say. Looks like a half glass of Bailey's and a beer makes me more social.

"Nora! I'm so glad you're here!" She gives me a hug, and I'm taken aback by how friendly she is.

"Yeah," I say. "Callum brought me. Callum Cassidy."

"I know Callum!" she says.

"And his friend Michael," I add, so it doesn't seem like I'm obsessed with Callum, which I only am a little.

She smiles and begins applying lipstick. "So," I say, trying not to be too obvious, "Callum's a good guy?"

Maeve laughs. "Yes, he's a good guy."

"Is he . . . single?"

Maeve carefully twists the base of her lipstick and replaces its cap. "Callum is . . . a good guy." She smacks her lips and fixes a smudge. "But I don't want you to, you know, get the totally wrong idea. He's incredibly friendly. He flirts with everyone. *Everyone.* That's not to say he doesn't like you—he probably does—but just . . . you know."

"Did you ever go out with him?" Of course she has. She's gorgeous and lives here, and he's come here every summer. I bet they're practically engaged.

"No! God, no. I've known Callum since I was a baby. He's like a weird younger brother who's actually older than me. But he went with my friend Fiona last year. They're still mates, but, you know, he hurt her. She got jealous, she broke it off."

"Oh." I'm not sure how I'm supposed to respond. I don't really need whatever this thing is with Callum to be a big deal. I'm only here for a few more weeks anyway. I just want to enjoy Ireland, not get caught up in some love triangle. How come in the books it's always the girl with two gorgeous and equally brave men pining after her? In real life it tends to be one boy who probably isn't that great to begin with surrounded by a handful of girls who've built him up to be the love of their lives. Even under the thumb of a dystopian Colony regime, Valentine Neverwoods doesn't know how good she has it.

"You should meet Fiona!" Maeve says. "She's here. Redhead. Probably one of dozens, but she's lovely. You'll like her."

"Yeah, sure," I say. "Listen, I'm going to . . ." I give a head-shrug and point, the universal sign for "get back out there."

"See ya in a bit!"

I don't spot Callum right away, so I stand by the periphery of the party, watching the bodies move and hearing the waves of laugher rise and fall in time to the music, now something with a bass beat that makes both the structure of the building and my rib cage vibrate.

Callum swings into view, doing the step-dance with a pretty redheaded girl who apears to be a good four inches taller than him. He doesn't see me; his face is frozen in a half-laughing smile. I continue clapping along with the music, wondering whether I should go up to him or wait for the song to end. When the song does end, I start making my way toward them, hoping to cut in, but Callum still doesn't see me. A new song begins, and he's dancing with the girl again.

"Let's dance," Michael says from behind me, and in a wave of relief, I accept. Michael has a helmet of dark hair and a slightly acned face, and I decide immediately that he's the type of person I could be instant friends with. We dance for another song, until I've forgotten all about Fiona and Callum and instead just start laughing involuntarily. Now I get why Kate Winslet decided to stick with Leo instead of her rich, guylinered fiancé: Irish dancing is the funnest thing I can possibly think of.

"Nora!" Callum calls out, heading over to me and Michael, his arm around the redhead. We're all winded and grinning. "Have you met my friend Fiona?" We shake hands. "Michael, mate, I saw your lady out for a smoke outside."

"Ah, thanks, I'll grab her a drink," Michael says.

"I'm going to grab another too," Fiona says, and the two of them head off toward the bar.

"Where've you been? I lost you," Callum says.

"Oh, just . . . you know . . . here." I smile and he smiles back, and he wraps one of his arms around my shoulder. It feels really, really good. Better than it should. He's wearing a leather coat that's impossibly soft and still smells like rain.

"Who's Michael's lady?" I ask.

"Maeve—you've met her, I bet. She's at the Deece too. Her parents run the place."

"Yes! I know Maeve!" *Her parents are Áine and Declain!* My brain is too busy firing off exclamation points to remember whether I said anything embarrassing about Callum in front of her. "I didn't realize she was dating Michael."

"They've been dating for around three years now. They're impossibly relaxed about the whole thing too. I don't think I've ever seen PDA. Michael's just so not that kind of guy. He's held this gang of us together over the years; he's kind of the heart of it."

"Are they your group chat?"

"Yeah—Michael, Maeve, Claire, Cameron, Jono, and me. Jono's in London for the summer, and Claire's in Dublin. That's the gang."

I wish I had a gang. There's something impossibly romantic about six friends who have known one another forever and share a massive group text even when they're separated.

"So you guys are like the TV show *Friends*?"

He laughs. "Yeah, I guess we are."

"So who would you be?"

"Well," he turns serious. "I s'pose Michael and Maeve are Ross and Rachel then, even though he's really more of a Chandler. Or Phoebe? Could a boy be Phoebe? Cameron is more like the Ross."

"So . . . you're Joey?" Of course. Handsome womanizer who likes sandwiches.

"Yeah, I guess so, although I'd like to think I'm not quite the dumb one."

A boy with a beard gets up on the stage and takes the mic, an acoustic guitar swinging at his waist. "All right now, gents, down another because we're singing next." He's joined on stage by Fiona, who's carrying a violin, and a boy with another stringed instrument that looks like a cross betweeen a banjo and a mandolin.

They start playing and singing, and everyone in the entire hall except me knows the words. "It's a folk song, sort of," Callum says. "One of those songs everyone just knows. You'll catch on."

And after the first chorus, I think I do. When the chorus hits, everybody shouts, "No, nay, never! No, nay, never, no more! Will I play the wild rover, no, nev-errrrrrrr! No more." Except after the first "No, nay, never" everybody gives four big claps. So it's something like, "No, nay, never!" [CLAP CLAP CLAP CLAP] "No, nay, never, no more!" [CLAP CLAP] "Will I play the wild rover, no, nev-errrrr! No more."

The words for the rest of the song elude me, but I defintely got the clapping down.

"It's like *Friends*!" I say to Callum once the song is over.

"Hm?"

I sing: "So no one told you life was gonna be this way" and then do the four claps. CLAP CLAP CLAP CLAP. I wait for his reaction. "There's a mashup waiting to happen!"

"I'm pretty sure the world isn't ready for your musical genius," Callum laughs. "But I fancy you anyway. Now, let me get you that promised drink."

Callum emits a pheromone or something that just makes me want to be around him, in the crook of his arm again, smelling his leather coat. Is that what pheromones do? It might be the beer (and the shot Fiona, Maeve, and I do later at the bar), but by the time Callum walks me back out to his truck, I'm floating, with "The Wild Rover" stuck in my head.

"No, nay, neverrrr!" I sing. Callum laughs. Even though the rain has stopped, the ground is still wet and spongy, and every surface is slick with water. The air smells like Callum. Then he presses me up against the driver's side door of his truck, and even though my back is getting soaked, he holds me there for just a minute, our faces close.

"Hi," I say.

"Hi," he says.

And I stare into his blue eyes for so long that I half-expect them to change color or morph like a gif somehow.

And then one of us leans in, and I'm not sure who, but we're kissing and it's perfect and his lips are soft and taste like beer but in a good way. I press into him harder, just a little, letting my leg slide slightly up his, denim on denim.

We break apart and smile.

"Michael!" Callum calls out as Michael and Maeve make their way out of the hall, hand in hand. "Mind driving? I had a few."

"As always, mate."

Callum throws the keys, and Michael catches them one-handed, kissing Maeve on the cheek in victory. "Need a ride?" he asks.

"Nah, I'm going to walk." She gives me a look like *I know that you were just totally macking on Callum Cassidy, and yes, I said "macking," but I'm cool enough to pull it off.* I give a shy smile back.

"All aboard!" Michael calls, hopping into the driver's seat.

Callum opens the door for me and insists I sit in front. I do, this time without argument. It's the same drunk feeling I had on the way here, only now my head is swimming for real: with the alcohol, with the heat from the barn, and with the memory of Callum's lips on mine.

17

I'M DRUNK, BUT I'm not *drunk* drunk. I've seen movies—I know what *drunk* drunk looks like: stumbling around, slurring words, texting exes. *Okay*, I think to myself. *Well, to be totally honest with myself, I do feel the strong and overwhelming urge to text my best friend's boyfriend whom I used to hook up with.* I think about texting Nick (thank you, Deece WiFi), and then it's done, a Facebook message eloquently reading, "heyyyyyyy." It's like I'm the evil little boy from that episode of *The Twilight Zone* where he sends people out to the ominous cornfield because he has creepy telepathic powers. He just needed to think something, and *bam!* it was done. That's how the message to Nick happens. It's like my fingers aren't even part of the equation. Straight brain-to-message technology.

The grass is dark and slick. The world is washed over with dimness like an old, forgotten painting. A hawk somewhere caws loudly.

I enter Evelyn's house and make it back up to my room without being too loud, I hope. It's twelve forty A.M., and though I'm forty minutes late, my beer-fogged brain tells me not to worry.

And then I see that the light in my mom's room is on.

"Hi," I say in her doorway. She's reading the Tina Fey memoir I bought her a few years ago for Mother's Day. Her T-shirt, the one from Dad's fortieth birthday party, has half a dozen holes along its edges. "Enjoying your book?"

"You're late," she says. "I waited up for you."

"I'm sorry. I didn't ask you to wait up."

"Of course you didn't ask me to wait up. I was worried about you!" She's yelling, but in a half whisper, trying not to wake Evelyn. The whisper-yell is almost scarier.

My mother yelling at me for coming home late from a party: What Lifetime Original Movie did we fall out of? At least she doesn't seem to realize I'm slightly *drunk* drunk.

"Are you *drunk*?" she whisper-screams.

Dammit.

"No. I had one beer." And another beer and a shot and then another beer. I don't want to get in a fight right now with her leaving so soon, so I come up with a plan: "Hey, Mom. There's no class tomorrow. Why don't you and I spend the day together? Just us."

She deliberates, taking a deep breath and pacing back and forth for a few steps. I don't realize I've been holding my breath. "Okay," she says finally, and I deflate with relief. "Just you and me. Now we both should get some sleep."

Evelyn made us a picnic, and even though the ground is still slightly wet from last night's rain, she tells us that it won't be too bad with a blanket. So, my mother and I sit on the top of a grassy hill overlooking Evelyn's and eating sandwiches with butter and ham (it's less gross than it sounds) and bags of an Irish brand of potato chips called Taytos. I realize that I have never seen my mother eat potato chips.

"This is new for you," I say.

"What do you mean?"

"Eating potato chips! Eating a sandwich!" My mother is the type of woman who pre-slices cucumber and red pepper to bring to work in Tupperware with organic hummus. It's part of her control freak nature.

The air smells different today: a little like mulch, but mostly like ocean. My mood buoys with every inhale.

"I can go with the flow!" she says and takes a big bite of her sandwich. "I've never had ham and butter before, though."

"Surprisingly good, right? They had little sandwiches like this at—" I manage to stop myself, but not soon enough. My mom gestures for me to finish my sentence. "Dad's wedding. I'm sorry, I didn't mean—"

"It's okay, Nora. Really."

I don't believe her, but at least she hasn't fallen apart. We pack up and begin walking back to the cottage. Suddenly, my mom stops, staring ahead in a stony silence. I flash back to the weeks after my dad left, when I would come home from school and see her sitting on the couch, staring blankly at whatever infomercial happened to be on the screen in front of her.

"Nora," she says finally. I can feel what's coming—she's going to start in again on how hard it's been since Dad left and how much harder it's going to be next year when I leave for college. I swallow hard and wait. There's not much I'm going to be able to say.

"How would you feel," she chooses her words carefully, her profile haloed by the sun, "if I were to stick around in Ireland a while longer?"

I just run my hand along the wicker handle of the picnic basket, back and forth, back and forth, so she jumps back in: "I've just been getting along so well with Evelyn, and it's been so nice to spend time with you."

"But what about—I mean, don't you have to get back to work?"

Her face darkens—she's clearly not pleased with my reaction. "I spoke to them already. It's fine."

"You . . . spoke to them already."

I say nothing else and head back toward the cottage. How does my mom continue to do this? To manipulate people and situations so that the chips fall in her favor? My trip has become her self-help vacation, her divorce therapy, her own little *Eat Pray Love*.

I laugh. It's all I can do. I laugh a bitter, hard, Disney-villain cackle and drop the picnic blanket, ignoring it as it tumbles down the hill like a stupid child in a nursery rhyme, and I swing around to face her. "Really?" I say. "So you're just sticking around. You're just *sticking around.*" I'm repeating myself like my brain is on tape delay, churning through the same few thoughts over and over again. "You realize what you're doing, right? You're manipulating me. *Again.*"

"Nora, you're blowing this a bit out of proportion."

"I'M NOT!" I shout, louder than I mean to. "I mean, the fact that you're here in first place and now that you want to stay longer . . . am I just supposed to be fine with all of this? If you were me, would *you* be fine with all of this?"

A cow looks up from the next field over, startled by my voice.

"I thought things were going well between us," she says, far too calmly. "I thought we were finally on the same page again."

"Grandpa's trip was one thing, but I got myself into this program, and I'm here to *work.*" I'm close to tears. "I really, really need to focus, and I can't be . . . worried or tied to anyone else right now. And you don't even support my art!"

She pauses and, to my surprise, takes both of my hands in hers. "I will not get in the way of your art, I promise. I know that the DCYA is a time for you to work, and I'm not going to get in the way of your focus. It's just been so nice being out off Evanston and on vacation. I can't remember the last time I went on a vacation! I know you need this, Nora, but I do too." She gives me a hopeful, pleading look, and I know I'm stuck.

"Just promise that you're not going to . . . distract me. I really, really need to focus on my art."

"I promise. It'll be like I'm not even here."

The cow has gone back to its chewing, bored by our interaction. Now we're left with the rumbling of distant thunder and the swishing sound we make with each step. My mother picks up the picnic basket. As we make our way down the hill, the air gets slightly thicker—full, I think, of things unsaid—and I can't smell the mulch or the ocean anymore.

18

AS IT TURNS out, the Deece does have more than one studio: A, B, C, and D are scattered along a single dirt road, with plenty of empty farmland in between where cows can be seen reclining behind distant fences on sunny days.

Monday, Wednesday, and Friday we're in Studio B with Áine, eight of us together, working at a single long wooden table like we're making a tableau of *The Last Supper*. It's my favorite time—the room takes on the heady smell of acrylic paint, and Áine blasts her heavy metal music in a language I'm almost positive isn't English.

We spent all of last week working on still-life paintings: Áine set bowls of fruit, skulls, wine bottles, and sweaters on the table and told us to paint whatever "spoke" to us. The Australian girl, Tess, told me she heard a rumor that we'd be working from live models our last week, although no one has wanted to ask Maeve whether it's true or not.

The real academia takes place in Declan's classes on Tuesdays and Thursdays. Unlike Áine, who focuses on practical application and experimentation, Declan teaches us the fundamentals of art through PowerPoint presentations. His are the only classes that don't take place in one of the studios; we meet in the basement of Áine and Declan's house, where a makeshift classroom and projector have been assembled.

It's amazing to me that the two of them ever got married. I've already come to dread Tuesdays and Thursdays, when we all file into his lair, where natural light has to claw its way in, and sit on uncomfortable stools all day. The first half of the lesson is strictly lecture, with Declan working on an actual chalkboard to teach us about linear form and the history of certain artistic movements. After lunch, we bring out our own sketchbooks and work through whatever repetitive assignment he gives us. "Repetition teaches your muscles! Art is as much about what your hands can do as what your head can do!"

Áine might tell you to add more shading or depth, or draw a line herself on your canvas that somehow makes the entire thing infinitely better, but no one has ever left one of her lessons feeling bad about their art.

Today, though, we're away from the mysterious Irish power couple of the art world. For the first time, we're told to go to Studio D. To my surprise, it's equipped with eight giant wheels, for sculpting, in two neat rows like the orphan girls in *Madeline* books.

"Oi," comes a voice from the back of the studio, and we see a girl in a tank top and two long pigtails haul a wad of clay up onto her own wheel. Her arms are muscular, like she's training to star in a new action-thriller alongside Matt Damon, and her ears look practically metallic from the sheer number of piercings she's managed to fit onto a relatively small area of flesh.

"I'm Bekka," she says. "And I'm going to teach you how to sculpt." She wipes her hand across her forehead, leaving a trail of gray-green clay on her skin. "First rule, don't be afraid to get messy."

One of the boys in the class, Rodger, strides forward toward Bekka's giant mound of clay. Rodger has a face locked in a perpetual smirk and a curl of hair frozen over his forehead like Clark Kent. If Rodger were in a movie, he'd play the pastel-sweater-wearing prep from across the lake trying to take over the camp populated by lovable misfits.

Rodger grabs a handful of clay. Bekka slaps it to the ground.

"Second rule," she says, "you're not ready to actually work with the clay until you know the fundamentals."

Rodger rubs his wounded hand as if it is still sore and slinks back into line.

"Oh, come off," Bekka says. "That didn't actually hurt."

She speaks with a heavy accent that could be Australian, but I'm not quite sure. She says she's a "kiwi," which doesn't exactly clear things up for me, but it's just amazing that a woman who doesn't look that much older than me can be teaching across the world and slapping jerks' hands down because she's just that badass.

Turns out, there are a lot of fundamentals. Bekka brings in tiny models of famous Roman sculptures, and she projects pictures from all around the world onto the wall and points out each one until we can all tell the difference between a Rodin and a Bernini in our sleep.

"Look at the way Bernini allowed the scene to be conveyed in a single instant, if you view the piece sideways," Bekka says, showing a projection of *Apollo and Daphne* on the white wall.

The sculpture shows Apollo, the Greek god of light and music, reaching toward the nymph Daphne with the full intention of nonconsensual activity. One foot in the air, one hand on her waist, Apollo is mid-chase. Daphne is looking back in fear, her eyes contorted with worry and her mouth slightly agape in a silent scream. Half of her body is being transformed into a tree, her final method of escaping her rape-y pursuer.

With a click, Bekka brings up a close-up image of Daphne's fingers, slightly elongated, branching into delicate laurel leaves.

Click. A close-up of bark creeping up Daphne's legs.

"We think of sculpture as static," Bekka says. "But it's an artist's way of capturing movement in the most profound manner. There's a story here: tension, suspense, and then resolution."

She uses the tiny model for emphasis. "Start at the back of the sculpture, and you just see Apollo pursuing. Then, you walk around counterclockwise," she says, twisting the model, "and you see Daphne—the fear on her face, the desperation. Finally, turn to the front, and you see the story's end: Daphne transformed into a tree. It's a three-act play in a single sculpture."

I almost want to clap at the end of the end of her mini lecture. I've never been remotely interested in sculpture before. The last time I sculpted, I was in elementary school, making hand-sized bowls by rolling out clay like snakes and coiling them. This . . . this is completely different.

Finally, once we've proven to Bekka (who I learn is actually from New Zealand) that we're sufficiently versed in the fundamentals, we get to touch the clay. "We're just doing bowls today," Bekka says, almost in warning, eyeing Tess, who has already built her sample of clay into a humanoid shape in the fourteen seconds since Bekka turned her back. Tess rolls her eyes.

"I've been making bowls since I was about four," Tess says in her thick Sydney accent. I expect Bekka to punish her for being so rude to a teacher, but instead she just flicks Tess's tiny figure and sends it crumpling into a clay puddle.

"And I've been sassing Aussies for a lot longer," Bekka says, and they both laugh.

The best part about class with Bekka is whether or not I'm terrible at sculpture makes no difference: There's no real way to tell. My bowl on the potter's wheel is elongated and slightly asymmetrical, but it looks beautiful nonetheless.

"That's great," Bekka says when she comes up behind me. "You have real hands for this. Just a little softer." She puts her hands over mine, like a platonic Patrick Swayze. "Here."

And like magic, my bowl gets better. She gives the piece dimension and an elegance that I hadn't seen before. One small change and things come together. A wheel amplifies every touch, making every gesture that much more important.

I leave her class covered in clay and glowing with pride.

"Hey!" Callum calls from his car when Tess, Rodger, and I come back from dinner. The car idles, the only one in a dirt parking lot. Maeve is already in the backseat with her legs in Michael's lap.

"We're going to figure out a way to get into the lighthouse," Michael calls through cupped hands. "Come on, hop in."

The three of us start running. Tess gets to the car first and pulls her body into the passenger seat, planting a wet kiss on Callum's cheek. I run through all the ways they could know each other, but I'm coming up empty. Rodger and I end up knee-to-knee in the backseat with Michael and Maeve.

Tess puts her feet on the dashboard and is nearly jolted through the windshield when Callum has to stop suddenly to let some ducks waddle safely across the road.

"Easy there, mate!" Tess says.

"It's just a good thing I'm driving instead of one of the Deecers, or we'd be eating duck for dinner," Callum says, winking at Tess. I suddenly notice how pretty Tess's blue eyes look and how Pinterest-worthy her braid is.

Maeve kicks the back of Callum's seat. "Hey! I'm a good driver!"

"Suuuuuuure you are," Callum says, looking back at me and smiling. "Do you want to tell Nora how you nearly drove us off the cliffs, or should I?"

When we finally make it to the lighthouse, it's almost dark. Michael cracks a tall can of Guinness and tosses one to Callum, who catches it with one hand.

"I'd give one to you, mate," Michael says to Rodger, "but Cromwell ruined this country, and the English caused the potato famine, so . . . retributions."

"It's a good thing I'm from *Wales*, then, mate," Rodger says and snatches the beer from Michael's hand. Michael raises an arm, giving the international signal for *touché*, and reaches in his bag for a third beer, which he offers to me. I decline. He shrugs, pops it open, takes a long swig, and then shares it with Maeve.

Tess is already halfway to the lighthouse, her long hair streaming behind her like the tail of a kite. "Come on, you buttwads, my grandma could make it quicker than you!"

Michael covers my ears. "The American isn't used to such harsh language."

I pull his hands down to his sides. "Oh, this American needs an education," I say.

Michael grins like a lunatic. "In that case, last one to the lighthouse is a buttwad."

He runs off, hand in hand with Maeve, who gives me an apologetic look over her shoulder before racing full speed ahead, her laugh echoing in the wind.

Callum swings back for me, and before I know what he's doing, he picks me up over his shoulder like I weigh ten pounds. "What do you say?" he calls up to his friends—*our* friends. "American in the ocean? I think the American goes in the ocean."

He wades forward as I shriek and pull at his arms until he's knee-deep in the water. Finally, he lets me down.

I make the completely mature decision to trip him, and he falls face-first into the water, but not before yanking me down with him.

Before long, Michael, Maeve, Rodger, and Tess abandon their own pursuit toward the lighthouse and join us in the ocean until we're all soaking wet and splashing each other.

"It's always locked anyway," Michael says dejectedly, looking at the lighthouse in the distance.

"Besides," Callum says, "the snacks and beer are in the car."

"That sounds like a much better plan," I say, dragging myself from the water, the weight of my clothes threatening to pull me back with every step.

The six of us sit, butts in the damp grass at the edge of the sand, in a semicircle looking at the water: Rodger, Maeve, Tess, Michael, and then me and Callum, his arm around me. The tide is so low that I can see the sand through the water, stippled with melting sunlight. We're all still damp with seawater and spilled beer.

"You going to miss us?" Tess asked suddenly. Her question is ostensibly directed at Maeve, who's seen probably a dozen classes of Deece students come and go, but it feels as though it's directed at all of us. What is our relationship going to be when we scatter back to our home countries, for college or careers, without seeing each other for daily studio time?

"Well, we're all Facebook friends," Michael says.

"You're all invited back to my place for my eighteenth birthday," Tess says. "It's going to be massive. Street-wide. A full rager."

I turn toward Maeve. "Do you keep in touch with other Deecers?"

"Sometimes," she says. "It gets harder when they go away, but I have a few friends I talk to every day. One in India. One in California. I dunno. A few."

And then Callum moves his mouth so close to my ear it's almost like he's kissing it. "We're going to stay in touch," he whispers, and the sensation of his breath on my skin is so electrifying that I can't help but giggle. Soon all six of us are giggling for no reason at all, and as the water fades into a deeper and deeper blue, I nuzzle up against Callum. "You better not forget me," I say.

And in a voice so quiet I'm not sure if I imagine it, he answers back: "I couldn't if I tried."

When I return to Evelyn's place, dripping wet, my mom doesn't say a word. She simply looks up from her book, sighs with a small smile, and goes back to reading.

"Try not to drip on the carpet!" Evelyn calls cheerfully from the kitchen.

The days of Deece pass in a blur—between meals, studio time, lessons, keeping in touch with Lena via sporadic and shallow Facebook messages ("off to rehearsal, hope you're having fun!—L"), and sulking quietly around my mom and trying not to let her see my notebooks, I have less time for Callum than I'd like.

I head to the studio after hours, with the goal of finishing work on an assignment for Declan— chalky pastels and tempera paint used together to create a waxy effect—when Callum comes through the door.

"I had a feeling I'd find you here."

I decide to play it cool and pretend like I haven't been thinking about him for days. I tilt my head toward my painting. "I think I might actually be getting close to not terrible at this!" I take a step back. The cow skull I've been painting almost looks three-dimensional. I've never painted anything like this, in this style, at home.

"You didn't answer your messages," Callum says, waggling his phone.

"I was working." I turn my phone off when I work. That was one of the lessons Declan gave us on the first day—eliminating distractions—but for once, he taught me something I already knew. I never paint when there's the possibility that my phone is going to light up and pull me away from a project right when I'm making a crucial line. Art is when I get to escape from the real world.

"C'mon," Callum says. "I'm taking you away."

"But I'm not done yet."

"It is"—he checks his phone—"eleven P.M. on a Friday night. If you don't come out with me now, I'm going to become incredibly depressed for the both of us."

"Fine. Let me just clean up."

Callum absentmindedly fingers a few of the brushes on the counter. "Your mum isn't going to care if you're out later than midnight, is she?"

I begin washing my palette in the stone sink and trying to get the pastel from my hands. The water runs rainbow for a few seconds. "No. Luckily, with her whole 'I'm staying in Ireland' thing, we have a pact where she's not allowed to comment on my life or life choices."

"Well, that's good," Callum says. "Because tonight your life choice is getting into a truck with a boy you barely know and letting him take you to a mystery location."

"When you put it like that, it does sound slightly problematic."

He smiles, and in this moment, I want to kiss him. I want him to rip my clothes off, and I want us to roll on top of the painting, the still-wet residue of my semi-decent cow skull rubbing off on our backs. Instead, I grab his hand, flick off the light to the studio, and say, "Lead the way."

"A cemetery?" I ask as we pull up outside the gates and Callum kills the headlights.

"Not just any cemetery," Callum says. "Well, yeah, kinda like any cemetery, actually." He grins.

I take his hand again, partly because I'm desperate for any physical contact with him and partly because we're at a cemetery in the middle of the night. I listen to the crunch of wet gravel beneath our feet, and as we walk along the tiny winding pathway through the dark grass, I try to catch the names on some of the tombstones. Most of the them are crumbling, too old for their words to be visible, their faces smoothed by time and weather. I see one mausoleum with the name CASSIDY carved in it, but I don't say anything.

After what feels like an hour of walking, Callum directs me to a bench underneath a tree wider than we are. All of the leaves look black in the darkness—the cemetery is lit only by a few lamps hovering somewhere in the distance. If we weren't surrounded by decaying bodies, it would be incredibly romantic.

"One of the oldest cemeteries in Ireland," Callum says.

"Really?" I say.

"I mean, probably, right? It sounds cool. I come here sometimes. Just to think. It's quiet."

"I like it."

"You can share it," Callum says. "It can be your place too."

"That's a very generous offer, Callum Cassidy."

"We superheroes are the giving and generous kind. Always looking out for humanity and the greater good, et cetera, et cetera."

I pull my backpack onto my lap to get it off the damp grass.

"What do you have in here anyway?" Callum says, and he opens the bag. "A notebook, classic, some pencils, sunglasses, a crumpled receipt from a Starbucks in Belgium—why did you go to Belgium, of all places?"

I laugh. "Honestly, I have no idea. My grandpa wanted me to? It sounded cool?"

"Belgium is a joke."

"I know, right?"

"But," Callum says, "not to be distracted! What else do you have . . . Chapstick, very practical. And . . ." He pulls out the second book in the Categories trilogy, *Blood Betrayed*. I brought it on the trip in case I needed something comforting to reread.

"I finished that one already. All of them, actually. Must have just left it in my bag." Does he think I'm dumb for reading this kind of book? I should have brought *Pride and Prejudice* or *Ulysses* or *Gravity's Rainbow* or something.

Callum flips the book in his hands. His hands are always moving. "Is it any good?" He begins reading out loud from the back cover. "'Valentine Neverwoods never believed she was special. At least not until the Test decided that she was the only one who'd be able to save the Colony from the sinister forces of the Citadel's power. With her childhood friend Ermias and the dark and mysterious Anthem—'" He turns to me. "I'm already lost."

"So, the Categories trilogy takes place in this dystopian future where, at sixteen, everyone in the Colony where they live has to take this Test that decides everything about their future. And while Val was taking it in the last book, she got a corrupted reading and figured out that the Citadel, who runs it all, has been corrupted. So now she's trying to overthrow the system."

"So . . . kind of like *The Hunger Games*."

"Yeah, sort of, but also not really?" I get a little embarrassed. "I mean, a lot of those stories are similar in certain ways, but they're all about growing up."

"What do you mean?" Callum cracks his knuckles and looks into my eyes like he actually wants to know the answer.

"I mean . . . how nice would it be if there were a Test to tell you exactly where you belong, a Test that could read every thought that's in your head and every experience you've ever had and all of your skills and be able to tell you: THIS. This is what you should do. This is what will make you happy. This is who you are."

"Well, no one knows who they are, exactly."

"I know, but you know . . . Read enough of these books and you can say, I get it—I'm a Gryffindor, or a Dauntless, or, like in the Categories books, an Academic or Artisan. If I were in the Categories books, they would have told me when I was sixteen if I was supposed to be an artist or not. And if it's not, then I wouldn't be wasting my time."

"Isn't it more fun just to do what you like and then see what you become later?"

"That's an optimistic way of looking at things," I say.

Callum straddles the bench so he's fully facing me. "I mean, this way's way better. You get to choose what you *want* to be. You don't need skills you were born with or permission. If you want to be an artist or whatever, just work harder than everyone else and become an artist!"

"You make it sound so easy. So what do you want to be?"

"I don't know," Callum says, and he swings his legs back around to the other side of the bench. "I kind of want to go into international law. Get out of Ireland."

"Are you applying for colleges outside of here?"

"Erm, a bit, yeah. You mean uni, right? Oxford's a long shot, but I'm also applying to Trinity and UNC in Dublin, and Wesleyan and Brown in the States."

"No way. I'm applying to RISD—Rhode Island School of Design. It's right next door to Brown."

"Ha! I didn't even know there was an art school up there! So why there?"

"Well, it's one of the best art schools in the country. Why Brown out of all the colleges—unis—in the States?"

"Well, I fancy Emma Watson quite a bit obviously, and she might come back for some reunions." I hit him gently on the side of his arm. "I mean, it's a great school! Ivy, yeah? And I like that they don't make you choose what you want to do right when you get there."

"Well, no colleges force you to choose exactly what you want to do right when you get there."

"In the UK they do! You apply for a specific program, and you can transfer if you really want, but you're locked into your program. Like, if you want to be a doctor, you apply to that program when you're eighteen, and then you're set."

"But no one knows exactly what they want to do when they're eighteen! That's not fair! People change their minds all the time—how are you even supposed to know what you're good at BEFORE you go to college?"

"Well," Callum says, "I guess that's why . . ." He consults the back of the book. "Miss Valentine Neverwoods is trying to overthrow the Colony."

"She's overthrowing the Citadel. The Colony is just where they live."

"Well, now I see why you like these books so much," Callum says.

"Why?"

"She's at a colony, you're at the Deece . . ."

"What do you mean?" I say. Is he trying to tell me the Deece turns into a fight-to-the-death for the title of who gets to be Áine and Declan's favorite?

Callum waits for me to get it, his eyes wide and expectant. "You know," he says finally, "Donegal COLONY for Young Artists. You applied here. You're an artist. That's your test assignment or whatever."

I laugh, and the sound echoes through the cemetery. A bat or a hawk or something gives a scratchy call. "Luckily this one isn't run by a totalitarian dictator."

"I don't know . . ." Callum says, smiling. "I've heard Maeve tell me some pretty harsh stories about Declan . . ."

"I'm so lucky to be here," I say without thinking.

"What do you mean, lucky?" Callum says. "You're really good. I mean, like, you got in here, right? And it's hard. They turn down loads of people every year."

My tongue hangs languidly in my mouth while I decide whether or not to tell him about my grandpa and my sneaking suspicion that it's easier to get into a program when your grandfather is a living treasure to the art world. But I don't say it. Instead, I grab the satchel off his lap and begin rummaging through it. "So, what's in your bag?" I say in a tone I'm hoping comes across as "flirty Kate Hudson in a romantic comedy."

"Ah!" Callum stands up and, with the flourish of a stage magician, pulls out a giant blanket and a handful of candy bars.

"I come prepared." He sweeps the blanket out on the ground and invites me to join him.

I read the names of the chocolates he brought. "Whispa? Toffee Crisp? Crunchie? *Dairy Milk?*"

"You don't have Dairy Milk in the States? It's Cadbury!"

I choose Whispa and take a bite. We definitely don't have a candy bar like it: thin strands of waxy chocolate in a rope so that it crumbles in your mouth. "I think we have Cadbury, but my mom isn't really the type to buy much candy. On Halloween, she gives out Goldfish."

Callum sits up. "She gives out *goldfish*?"

It takes a minute, and then it clicks, and I'm laughing so hard I don't even care if it makes me have a double chin or snort like a drunk cow. "Goldfish. Like the crackers. Little crackers we have in America shaped like little fish."

"Well," Callum says, "I would have preferred if you gave away pet fish."

We sit for a while, watching the reflection of the moon bounce off the headstones and leave lens-flare patches on the grass. The chocolate has left me in a fuzzy haze, like my usual brain programming has been replaced by white noise on an old television set.

"It's late," I say finally, after we've been lying on the ground for a while, his head in the crook of my neck and his arm around my waist. I check my iPhone: two fourteen A.M. "Are we spending all night in a cemetery? We should be telling ghost stories."

"Mmmhmmmmm mmhmmmmhm," Callum says into my hair.

"I should get back," I say, but maybe I don't actually say it. Maybe I just think about saying it.

My eyes get heavy, and Callum is so warm and smells like grass and paint. I fall asleep with his arm as my pillow.

"Mummy, they're moving!"

I moan. I'm not entirely sure where I am or why the sun is so bright or why my shoulder is so sore. A little boy shrieks.

"Mummy, mummy—they're moving!"

I open my eyes just enough to see a boy waddling off toward his mother, shooting terrified glances back at me and Callum every few steps.

"Morning," Callum says, flipping over onto his back.

"We fell asleep," I say stupidly. And then I remember that morning breath exists and try to tilt my head slightly away from Callum's face. "Oh my god," I say and begin scrambling to stand up, grabbing my bag. "We fell asleep."

"Yeah, yeah, we did," Callum says, closing his eyes again.

"*We fell asleep!*" I say again, and the urgency in my tone rouses Callum from his attempt at the metaphorical snooze button. "My mother is going to flip out."

"I thought you said she's not allowed to comment on your life."

"She's not, but . . ." I try to explain things as best I can. "But, I mean, I just stayed out all night in Ireland. In a cemetery. Won't your parents worry?"

He shrugs a shoulder. "My da' doesn't know where I am half the time. He trusts me to take care of myself."

I don't respond. My stomach is churning with rage and

anxiety and maybe something like a full-on crush, but clouded by the first two emotions, it's hard to tell.

"Look," Callum says, "I didn't mean to cause a problem. I just . . . I mean . . . lemme drive you home." He re-laces his shoes and begins packing up the blanket.

The toddler who thinks we're zombies hides behind his mom until we exit the cemetery, me leading like a woman on a mission and Callum stumbling after me.

19

IN THE END, Alice went far easier on me than she should have, by all accounts. I got a lecture, an "I was *so* worried about you, you have no idea!" and after I promised to never be out later than midnight again without telling her, she pulled me into a hug and told me how angry she was, still hugging me. It was a distinctly non-Alice experience. I have to imagine the sea air or all the greenery, or else the time away from work, has had a calming effect on her, not to mention Evelyn, who let her know that the children from the Deece are known to stay out all night together, and this was a perfectly normal occurrence.

When I leave to meet Maeve in the studio (after a long, long nap and a cup of Evelyn's jasmine tea), I tell my mom I love her, and she says she loves me too, still shaking her head like she can't believe she had to survive the torture of worrying about me all night.

* * *

We're carving linoleum plates. In my head, the image I'm trying to carve looks perfect—a cup of coffee swirling with steam. I can picture it so clearly, but then when my hands try to scrape the picture out of the rubbery linoleum, it becomes warped and childish. This is already my second plate—with the first one, I pressed too hard, and the knife went all the way through, ruining it.

"Try to make longer, more shallow troughs, like this." Maeve puts her hand on mine and demonstrates the right amount of pressure. Already, with just one stroke of Maeve-assisted carving, my plate looks significantly better. But before I can feel even the slightest bit good about my piece, I peek over at Maeve's, and any semblance of self-esteem I had disappears like eraser residue being blown off a page. Maeve's plate depicts the face of a Greek god representing wind, his cheeks full with effort, his breath curling around him in gusts as he blows. My little lopsided coffee cup looks pathetic.

"Have you made these before?" I ask.

"Actually, no," Maeve says. "My mum asked me to try it out before the class does them Monday. When we finish with the plates, we'll roll them in ink and then press them like stamps."

"Oh. Cool." *So this all just comes naturally to her.*

I put down my small knife and watch Maeve work for a few minutes, the way her wrist flicks around the plate as if it has a life of its own, the look of placid concentration on her face. She's gifted. That's the thing I need to wrap my head around. I might be good, and I might work hard and become better, but

I will never be better than someone like Maeve, who has the sort of effortless talent that people talk about in speeches at lifetime-achievement award ceremonies.

But you got into the program, a little voice whispers in my head. *They wouldn't have accepted you to the Deece if you didn't show potential—if you weren't actually, truly talented.*

But your grandfather is Robert Parker, another voice from somewhere dark coos. *They probably only let you in because they thought you'd add prestige to the program. Or because they thought he'd donate. You're nothing but a name to these people.*

I stare at my own plate again for a few seconds. Every line seems wrong. I keep hoping that if I stare long enough, the picture will morph into something that looks as good as I want it to. What superpower is that? The ability to make things as good as you want them? Oh, right: *talent.*

Just as I pick up my knife to try again, maybe add some shadow, the wooden studio door swings open and clangs against the wall.

"Nice to see you, Cal," Maeve says, not looking up from her plate.

Callum swaggers up behind her and gives her a kiss on the cheek. I remind myself that he's just like that with everyone. He's Joey from *Friends*. "I thought I'd find you ladies here. On a *Saturday*. When you don't have class."

"We," Maeve says, "are testing out a new project for Áine and Declan."

"Teacher's pet," Callum says and sidles over between us to look at our work. He takes on the voice of a cliché snooty art gallery director. "Very nice," he says toward Maeve's work. "*Ve-ery nice.* Ah! And what do we have here?" He brings his nose almost to my plate. "Masterly use of lines and perspective. The coffee cup is obviously a metaphor for colonization in South America, yes?"

"But of course," I reply in my own snooty artist voice. "I thought that was *obvious.*"

Maeve giggles. "You're just jealous you're not allowed to play with knives," she says.

"It's true," Callum says, picking up one of the extra knives and twirling it in his fingers. "I've always wanted to master the art of using a knife the size of a fingernail to carve up a piece of plastic."

If I wanted my plate to look better before, now that Callum is here I'm wishing about ten times harder. Callum liked me in the first place because he thought I was a talented artist, and now here he is in the studio, looking back and forth between my plate and Maeve's, getting firsthand, empirical evidence that I'm average, at best. Maybe if I just go over the outline of the mug one more time, deeper, it'll look kind of art deco . . .

I cut all the way through the linoleum again. "*Fuck.*"

Maeve and Callum are too busy joking about something Michael did years ago even to notice how frustrated I am. I try not to let it show. I feel like I'm about to cry, and all I can think about is getting far away from Callum so he doesn't see that my cry-face is uglier than Kim Kardashian's.

"I'm going to do a painting," I say. They both look at me.

"I forgot that I was supposed to make one for Grandpa," I add quickly.

"Do you want me to press your plate for you?" Maeve asks.

"No," I say, too fast. "It's garbage, really." And before she or Callum can protest, I throw the ruined plate away, grab my bag, and head out the still-open studio door.

My strap gets caught on the doorknob, and they're both silent, watching me while I struggle with it for a few seconds.

"Okay," I say when I finally yank myself free. "Bye." And as I head out, the tears come quick.

I take my canvas and paints up the craggy coast until I can see the lighthouse in the distance, and I set up my easel in the grass. I'll paint a landscape. Grandpa didn't give me an assignment for Ireland, assuming that I'd be doing enough art at the colony, but I still feel the need to make something for him, to show him how grateful I am here and how much better I am after even a few weeks of expert direction. Back home, I never drew landscapes—they seemed like the type of boring art that ends up on the wall of a dentist's office. But after a lecture that Declan gave us on J.M.W. Turner, I'm suddenly fascinated by the idea of painting the water. Turner painted turbulent seas and ships fighting to remain upright. Declan talked to us about the way he used light to highlight certain areas of the canvas and create contrast between the harsh reality and the way people dream they might be.

The sea could be dark and stormy and turbulent and terrible, but there, in the corner of the canvas, there's a ray of light coming out through the clouds, piercing the painting like a sword. It's like he was able to paint the confusion and anxiety that goes on inside a person's head. Maybe I can too.

I've never painted water before, or at least I've never painted water like this before: the sea spanning out to the horizon, ebbing with light and dark spots and tiny plopping fish and capping waves that crest and disappear. I put everything that's bothering me in this painting: My fears that my mom can't seem to get a life of her own are represented in a looming wave that's ominously close to crashing; my anxiety about not being a good enough artist are the craggy cliffs by the shore, casting a shadow on the rest of the work; and my loneliness is in the tiny sailboat I paint in the distance, a ship that's not actually there but only in my imagination, manned by a girl who decided to leave all of her expectations behind and just try to live on her own. Maybe if my mom could empathize with this more, our relationship would be defined more by interactions like the one we had this morning and less by conversations that always turn into fights.

"Hey, Picasso!" Callum climbs up the hill behind me.

Just seeing him is enough to make me smile involuntarily. I wish I were the type who could hold a grudge, but I can't help myself. My stomach does an entire gymnastics floor routine. Silver medal to America!

"I'm painting the sea," I say back. "You should be saying, 'Hey, Turner.'"

"And imagine you as Timothy Spall? Never."

"Excuse me?"

He's so casual. He's acting like I didn't just storm out of the studio like a maniac. He plops down in the grass and crosses his legs. "Timothy Spall played Turner in the movie *Mr. Turner*. And you two look nothing alike."

"You watch a lot of movies."

Callum cracks his knuckles. "Well, I've spent a lot of time on buses traveling back and forth between Donegal and Dublin. Visiting Mum, then Dad. Trying to make nice." He cracks the knuckles on his other hand. When anyone else does that it drives me crazy, but for some reason, when Callum Cassidy does it, it's the sexiest thing alive.

I sit down in the grass next to him. "How long have your parents been divorced?" I ask, a bit worried that I'm overstepping my boundaries.

"Since I was four," he says, looking out toward the water. He doesn't elaborate.

"I get it," I say, scooting just a little bit closer to him. "My parents got divorced two years ago. My dad just got remarried. I think it's screwed up my mom."

Callum doesn't say anything.

"Oh," I add, "and my dad married my former math teacher."

He still doesn't look at me, but he does smile, and his hand inches closer to mine.

"My dad thinks that after uni I'm coming straight back here to work on the farm with my uncles," he says. "My mum hasn't told him I'm applying to law programs. He'd be furious—he thinks I want to be just like him."

"And you don't?"

"He's never left Ireland in his entire life! He has lived in the same house since he was born. I just . . ." He trails off and looks at me. "What's your dad like?"

"Well, the truth is, my dad isn't even my biological dad."

"What do you mean? You were adopted?"

I start slowly. The only person who knows about this is Lena, but I feel so comfortable with Callum that I want him to know everything about me. "My parents got married when I was three. My mom got pregnant with me when she was in college, and she dropped out to take care of me. Then she met my dad."

"But you still call him your dad?"

"Well, yeah. He's my dad. He raised me. He legally adopted me when he married my mom, and he's still my dad even though they got divorced."

"But do you know who your real dad is?"

"My dad is my real dad. The other guy is like . . . I don't know, like a sperm donor. My mom said if I wanted to get in contact with him when I was sixteen I could, but . . . I don't know. I have a dad. I never really felt the need to meet some stranger who shares half of my DNA."

We're quiet for a few minutes, just holding hands, looking at the water. I feel Callum's thumb trace up my palm and then back down. He turns to me, grinning.

"So, how weird was it that your dad married your math teacher?"

"So weird. But as bad as it was for me, I don't think it can compare to how my mom reacted. She walked around the house like a zombie for a full month before the wedding. I swear, the only time she opened her mouth was to tell me to choose a more practical career than being an artist."

"She doesn't want you to be an artist? But you're so good!"

"I mean, I kind of get it," I say. "She's had to take care of me since she was, like, twenty-two, and my grandpa is an artist and didn't become successful until he was already old, so she was really on her own for most of it. And now that Dad left, she has to make sure I have everything, and it's hard, y'know? I think she doesn't want me to have to go through that. She wants me to always be able to take care of myself."

Callum kisses me, soft, right on the lips, his mouth parted just enough to let through a hint of wetness. He's close enough that I'm filled with his smell: peppermint toothpaste and wet ground and clay. He pulls away, just an inch, and I can feel his cheek soft against mine. "I have a feeling you're always going to be able to take care of yourself, Picasso," he says quietly, right into my ear.

I am weightless. Dizzy in the best possible way. Desperate to keep him this near to me forever, his voice always so close to my ear that it sends tingles through my brain, neuron to neuron, firing back and forth until I can't think of anything except him, that smell, that taste.

Why can't all of life be like this? I make a mental promise to try to paint something that's able to capture this moment—when you open up to your crush and he opens up too, and then the two of you lie in the grass listening to the water, waiting for the moment when you can kiss each other again.

20

IT'S JUST ME and Bartholomeow at five A.M. in Studio A, the earliest I've ever voluntarily done anything in my entire life. I was up even earlier, consumed by eagerness to begin a painting that would sum up how I felt about Callum. Free studio time is a *privilege*, Áine reminded us at the beginning of the session, a privilege given to students in their last week of the program to display the skills they have gained and apply them within their own creative framework. Whatever that means.

Áine talks so much about the link between emotion and art. Thinking about the quadruple backflip my stomach landed when I saw Callum come up the hill by the cliff, I know that he's my key. The painting is going to be abstract—I know that much—but the details of it aren't quite perfect. I decide to make the canvas green, like the grass we were lying in, but I try to swirl a dry brush in the paint while it's still wet on the canvas in order to create texture. It's something Declan showed us a few days ago.

I look over at Maeve's canvas; hers already looks close to finished. It's a self-portrait done all in orange, her features blocked into cubist geometry. It's not enough that Maeve has to be a gorgeous painter; she's also plain gorgeous.

I force myself to rip my eyes away from her canvas and instead look at the words Áine painted in curlicue letters on the studio wall: THIS ABOVE ALL: TO THINE OWN SELF BE TRUE.

You got it, Polonius. I turn back to my own canvas, which, in the previous six and a half seconds, seems to have gotten far worse. But I take a deep breath, get lost in the heavy metal music, and paint.

"Start winding down," Áine calls a few hours later, turning down the music. Bartholomeow weaves between our feet, rubbing himself against us as if he knows he deserves a reward for not distracting us while we were working.

My painting isn't perfect, but it's definitely pretty good. It feels good to break out of my rut and create the kind of art that could actually be in a museum rather than on a Tumblr page. I've never painted anything abstract before, but with every heartbeat I'm replaying the words Declan emphasized the other day: structure, using the space on the canvas, creating contrast, having a visual focal point. The words that were once so confusing and vague now seem to make sense. I'm thinking back to how I felt with Callum and putting it on the canvas. Maybe this is what being an artist is. Maybe I actually can do it.

Áine paces behind us, commenting on our work. Tess tore

up old newspapers and painted them onto the canvas, creating a really interesting texture.

"That's wonderful," Áine says. "I can't wait to see how this comes along."

Tess beams. Hers is good, but I'm secretly impatient to hear what Áine says once she gets to me. My improvement is obvious. This is the best thing I've done since I've been here. It's like my brush is acting on its own, just swirling colors and patterns in ways I couldn't have even fathomed before this program.

"Nora," Áine says, and she swallows once. "Hmm."

Her beaded necklace jangles ominously. Someone coughs.

"What do you think?" I ask.

"Well. I think you might be able to add some depth."

Depth? What does that even mean? This is an abstract paint-ing. What kind of depth?

"It's abstract," I say.

"Yes, I can see that."

I don't say anything, so she continues.

"I'd say that if you're really serious about making artistic progress in the long haul, you have to sacrifice immediate results for the good of creating something worthwhile that takes a little longer."

Tess looks over sympathetically, and I want to punch her in the face. I want to punch everyone in the face.

"Oh" is all I can manage to say.

"It's not bad!" Áine says quickly, reading my face. "I just think you should refocus on exactly what sort of artist you want to be."

"Oh," I say again.

"I'm just anticipating you hitting an upper limit to the amount of progress you'll be able to make if you keep thinking of art as so . . . linear."

I don't know what her words mean, or maybe I've just tuned them out, shut down my brain against someone actually saying what the tiny voice in the back of my head has been whispering to me my entire life.

I haven't heard Áine criticize anyone's work yet. The harshest thing she's said is when she told Rodger that he should use a warmer color palette on his sunrise. And now she's practically telling me that I shouldn't be an artist. I fight the instinct to splatter my palette on the canvas and ruin it completely. Áine gives me a smile, like she did me a favor, and moves on to look at Maeve's fucking perfect painting.

My eyes and cheeks burn. If I had a magic genie, my first wish would be to sink through the floor and disappear completely. My second and third wishes would be the exact same thing, just to make sure he heard me. I know if I stay in the studio, I'll cry. I have to get out.

"I don't feel well," I mutter, and I grab my canvas and run toward the studio door, getting wet paint all over my T-shirt. I don't care. All that matters now is getting as much distance from Áine and the studio as physically possible. I'm running from something inevitable. *I don't have what it takes to be an artist.*

Bartholomeow trots behind me, and I resist the urge to kick him. I make it out of the studio and walk down the eerily silent hall until I burst outside.

"*I spent twenty years learning to paint like Raphael...*" I think back to the slides Declan showed us in workshop of Picasso's early work. By the time he was a teenager, Picasso was sketching photorealistic bodies and painting portraits that looked like they were done by a Renaissance master. I'm seventeen, and I can't even do an abstract painting. All I'm good for is little cartoons on the Internet. I almost have to stop myself from laughing. Some of my most popular posts on Ophelia in Paradise are cartoonified versions of famous characters and paintings: *Mona Lisa*, *The Scream*, Grandpa's *The Reader and the Watcher*. That's all I'll ever be good for—not creating anything original, just sucking like a parasite on artists with real vision and hoping that my mediocre ability to use a stylus on an iPad can get me a few hundred responses from strangers online.

I see it clearly: If I decide to be an artist, I'm choosing a life in Evanston, commuting to my job making pamphlets and tweeting for the marketing department of some soulless company that makes honey barbecue peanuts or yoga pants for dogs. I will wear a wardrobe from Ann Taylor that I don't iron often enough, and I'll join a gym that I'll never go to, living at most forty minutes from the home I grew up in, able to drive back at a moment's notice to take care of my mom whenever she gets lonely or wants me to be there for dinner.

I don't realize how hard I'm crying until I stop running and gasp for breath. I must look like a mess: dripping with tears and snot, covered with paint. And I have nowhere to go.

Even if I wanted to, I couldn't go back to the cottage to talk with my mom; Evelyn took her on a trip to Galway, and they won't be back until tonight. Maeve is still in the studio. The only person I want to see now is Callum. He had so much faith in my work, and the painting was supposed to represent something we had together. He'll understand it, maybe—or even if he doesn't, he'll hold my hand and make me forget all about Áine and my nightmare of spending the rest of my life in a cubicle, drinking lukewarm cups of coffee and saving up vacation days to squeeze in a week to see the rest of the world before returning back exactly where I started.

I don't know where Callum is, but I have a hunch. Even if he's not there, I want to go back to the spot in the cemetery where we spent the night. I want to sit on that stone bench and look at the painting I made to represent the two of us together.

My heart swells when I see a figure on the bench—Callum is there. He'll put his arm around me, and I'll close my eyes in the crook of his soft leather coat, and he'll tell me that I'm not hopeless.

The cemetery seems empty except for him, facing away from me, his shadow bigger than I would have expected up against the tree. I hear female laughter from somewhere I can't quite place, which seems odd because I haven't seen anyone else in the cemetery. And then I get closer, and my throat tightens up, and I forget to swallow. I see the mass of Callum's dark curls, and I see long, red hair leaning against his shoulder, in the crook of his soft leather coat, where I should be. Their backs are to me, and when I hear the girl—*it's Fiona, it has to be Fiona*—laugh again, the sound is like a weapon, hurting my head and tightening my chest.

All I can think of is getting out of the cemetery without

them seeing me. The worst thing in the world right now would be them turning to me, Callum with the shadow of his falling smile on his face, trying to pretend everything is okay, that he wasn't just sitting in our spot with his arm around his ex-girlfriend. And Fiona would have to look mock concerned, maybe put on a condescending, exaggerated frown. *Oh boohoo, the little American girl with a mucus-green streak in her hair thought she was something special? Callum likes gorgeous redheads, not mediocre wannabe artists.*

The last time I felt this way was when Lena texted me that she and Nick had hooked up, and then an hour later, when Nick texted to tell me he was now going out with Lena. I made him swear not to tell her what happened between us, and he swore, but now every time I think of Lena I imagine her furious at me for keeping this secret, sitting with Nick, them laughing together about how pathetic I am, how I had sex with Nick thinking that he'd be interested in me and how he ignored my texts for the next four days because he thought I was great, really, but he just wasn't interested in me like that.

And now Callum is back with Fiona. I run away. I'm still holding the painting, I realize—the one I made to represent how I felt with Callum. The corner of it digs into my side. From far away, I think I hear someone call my name, but it's too late; I'm already running as fast as I can toward the cottage, throwing the painting I made into the dumpster behind the studio with a satisfying clang.

The clang is still ringing in my ears when the crying stops.

21

OH, THESE WERE the moments angsty pop music was built for. I imagine when Taylor Swift wrote "Forever and Always" she knew that somehow, years later, a girl would be alone in a cottage on the rural north coast of Ireland and be blasting it on her laptop speakers while she mixes together sugar, oil, cocoa powder, and flour in a mug and eats the resulting brownie-batter monstrosity straight out of said mug with a spoon. And, for that matter, why would Thirty Seconds to Mars ever have recorded "Kings and Queens" if they didn't know that I, Nora Parker-Holmes, would be singing it alone, dead sober, while drawing doodles of sad girls lying on couches and standing in showers and hiding under blankets?

By the time I hear my mom and Evelyn unlocking the back door of the cottage, I'm already hoarse from singing and nauseated from the makeshift desserts I've poured into my gullet. I'm sitting in my bed, wearing a tear-stained sweatshirt and rereading the first book in the Categories trilogy, *Blood Chosen*, hoping I can disappear within the familiar worlds, rejoining Val in her oppressive, comfortable, easy Colony where the boys are always handsome and love you more than anyone else. I'm just at the part where Val is talking to Ermias about how nervous she is for the Test when my mom opens the door to my room.

"I'm okay," I say, even though she didn't ask me anything. "I mean, hi."

I peek out from under the blanket, and she gives a sad smile and sits at the end of the bed. I think she's going to mention the half dozen mugs I left in the sink covered with chocolate powder, but she doesn't. She just strokes my hair, and I begin to cry.

"Did I ever tell you about the time I went to Paris as an undergrad?" She wipes a tear from my cheek.

I attempt to blow my nose on my sleeve, and she pretends not to be grossed out.

"I was a junior, and I was enrolled in an all-French-language program, even though I could barely speak French. And I wanted to be a writer or a lawyer even then, and I was reading so much that I basically kept to myself the entire time. Other kids in the program were going to bars and parties and making friends, and I stayed in the dorm, trying to read Proust in French and failing terribly. I wasn't as smart as you are."

I try to protest, but she puts up a hand to quiet me.

"And then one day, a British author was hanging around the dorms. And he was"—she pauses—"not quite well-known yet, although that's since changed. He was a few years older than me, and I thought he was charming, like any boy on a motorcycle would have been at the time."

I struggle to imagine my mother, whom I've never seen drive above the speed limit, on the back of a motorcycle.

"And when he took me out, it felt like I was finally getting the *real* Paris experience. I had been hiding away for two months, scared to go out alone into the city. But this man—boy, really—thought I was worth going out with, so *I* thought I was worth going out with. Do you understand?"

I nod, but I'm not sure I do.

"I didn't know who I was yet," she continues. "And I let someone else try to tell me. Or, rather, I let someone else's feelings for me affect how I felt about myself."

Her being here, stroking my hair, reminds me of being in elementary school, home with the flu. I feel guilty and grateful at the same time. "It's not just Callum," I say between gasps. "It's this whole art thing. And Nick. And just everything."

My mom doesn't say anything. She keeps stroking my hair. And then, after wiping my nose on the blanket, I manage to get it out. "It is Callum." I can't articulate any more. If I don't say it, it won't be real, and everything will reset to two days ago, when I had a crush on him and he wanted to spend time with me and everything was filled with possibility. "Tell me how the Paris story ends," I say.

My mom sits, quiet for another minute before she opens her mouth to speak again. "I spent the summer trying to be what I thought this boy wanted me to be, and in the end, when he moved on, I was heartbroken. But the world kept spinning. Life kept going, and it brought me something more powerful and important than anything else I've done. Something that's defined me and given me purpose. It brought me you."

My heart feels like it's swollen like a sponge in water. I have no idea how something the size of a ham fits inside my rib cage. I can't hold it in anymore. I have to say it out loud. And when I say it, it becomes real. "I saw Callum with another girl."

She's quiet for a few moments.

Finally, she clears her throat.

"You're going to meet so many wonderful people in your life, and travel to so many wonderful places. Paris, and meeting a stranger, and falling in love, however briefly, was all part of the experience that led me here, to you, to being your mother. Forget about Callum for now. Your journey is just beginning, and I promise you, it's going to be spectacular."

Instead of responding, I sob, and my mom holds my head in her lap like she did when I was young.

"If you can't let him go, talk to him. Communicate. But just know this: No one will ever complete you. You need to make sure you're complete on your own."

"I used to feel complete when I thought about being an artist. And now I feel like a failure."

"Do you realize what an honor it is to be selected for this program? Out of every young artist in the world? Here's the truth: There are no multiple-choice tests in real life to tell you what job you're supposed to do or whom you're supposed to date or marry. All you can do is listen to your gut. What makes you happy? Who do *you* want to be? And the best thing about life is that you don't need to limit yourself to just one category."

I can't smile, but I can turn to see her, and for the first time all trip, I'm genuinely grateful she's here. "I love you, Mom."

"I love you too, Bunny."

She hasn't called me that since I was little, and I smile in spite of myself, tears dripping into my mouth. It's all very gross, objectively. If there has been any revelation in all of this, it's that I am definitely not a pretty crier. I am a very, very ugly crier, and goddammit, I'm okay with that.

I sniff, hard. "Do you maybe want to take a weekend trip to Belfast with me? It's not far. And I hear it's really cool."

"I'd love that," my mom says. She goes into the bathroom and returns with a wet cloth. "Now let me just get this dried chocolate off your face."

That night I dream about taking the SATs again, but the only possible answers are Mother, Artist, Laborer, and—for some reason—Callum. Legolas is leading me through the Brussels city center and saying that since the test was indecisive for me, I need to make a choice for myself now. I keep saying no, no, no, just give me more time. Nick is laughing at me, and my mom is at the top of the town hall, but she's dressed in one of Declan's polka-dot suits, and she's crying and then I'm crying, and when I wake up, my pillow is wet, but I'm not certain whether it's from tears or drool.

Her advice makes sense. I'm going to talk to Callum and just lay out how I feel and, painful as it might be, how I felt when I saw him with Fiona. And however he feels, I'm not going to let it change how I feel about myself. Already I feel the tear that Nick made in me slowly and painfully filling in. But the fact that he's dating my best friend and could probably destroy our friendship any minute by telling her the secret I've kept for six months is something I can't deal with now. What I can deal with is Callum. And continuing to work as an artist.

My mom gave me good advice. And yet . . . she's still here, hiding in a cottage in Ireland, two years after her divorce. Whatever she's feeling, it's something that can't be helped with a pep talk and YA-novel metaphor.

22

RODGER AND TESS have decided that they know how to break into the lighthouse, and they've deemed me worthy to join them on their quest.

"I heard there's relics in there from the revolution, back when they used the lighthouse as an armory," Rodger says, his face deadly serious.

Tess looks at me and winks. "I hear it's where they hid the Kennedy Treasure—y'know, the money the Kennedy family made from bootlegging during America's Prohibition era when they wanted a safe place to store it, far away from suspicion," Tess says.

"A'ight, but why would the 'Kennedy Treasure' be hidden in Donegal when the Kennedys were from down near County Wexford?" Rodger answers, his face gone full smug.

"Exactly!" Tess says. "Even further away from suspicion." Tess and I laugh, and Rodger rolls his eyes.

"Anyway," I say, "Rodger, how do you know where the Kennedys are from? You're from England—they're not your people!"

"I," Rodger begins, "am from *Wales*. How do you not know *that* information?"

Tess races ahead of us on the beach. "Ooooh, ignorant American at it again!"

"Ignorant American: World's Lamest Superhero!" I call up to her and run as fast as I can, even though with her long legs she's already a speck in the distance. Of course, just mentioning superheroes makes me think about Callum, and the laughter catches in my throat.

Rodger catches up to us. "You do know I'm from Wales, right? Not England. I just want to make that very clear. There's a difference."

"Okay," I say and place my hand over my heart. "I promise never to make that mistake again. On Kennedy's grave."

"Good," Rodger says.

"Now that that's settled," Tess says, "what are you going to do with your share of the treasure?"

"Campaign for Welsh independence," Rodger says.

"I want a pet shark," Tess says. "Nora?"

"Probably pay for college. My grandpa is going to help with it, but I know that puts my mom in a weird position. I mean, I know she wants me just focusing on school so I don't have to be working two jobs while I'm there, but I don't like the feeling of owing someone, you know? Even if it's my mom. Or grandpa."

Tess and Rodger are both silent for a minute.

"Practical," Tess says finally.

Rodger pulls out a Swiss Army knife. "All right," he says. "Let's do this."

"We're not going to get in, like, a colossal amount of trouble for this, are we?" Tess asks.

"Who knows?" Rodger answers.

Like a hallucination, I see Callum up the shore, skipping rocks. Alone.

"Is that Callum?" Rodger asks. "Hey, Callum!" Callum looks over and gives a wave, then goes back to throwing flat rocks into the water and failing spectacularly to get them to skip.

"I'm going to go over and talk with him," I say. "I'm sorry, I won't be long."

Rodger scoffs. "Is this a lovey-dovey thing?"

"No," I say. "Well, maybe. Probably not."

"Practice safe sex!" Tess says. "Wait! What about your share of the treasure?"

I'm already walking down the beach toward Callum. "I'm ninety-nine percent sure the real treasure was friendship all along!" I say back.

Callum sees me coming but doesn't stop throwing rocks. "Hey," he says.

"Hey," I say. "You're really, really bad at that."

"Well, maybe that's why I need practice." He tries one more, and it lands in the water with a heavy *plunk*. I try one, and it skips four times gracefully.

"My grandpa taught me," I say with a shrug. "Lake Michigan."

Callum sighs and walks up farther toward the shore. He doesn't invite me to come along, but I do anyway. He's acting distant, and it's making my heart hurt like a physical symptom that I could type into WebMD and learn that the Internet thinks I have a rare tropical disease. I hear a metallic clunk echo from down the beach, followed by cheers.

"Rodger and Tess must've gotten into the lighthouse," I say.

"Oh?"

I'm tempted just to run away, to let Callum walk up the beach and turn around to realize that I'm already gone, I'm back with friends who laugh with me and joke about hidden treasure and don't cuddle up with their ex-girlfriends in the exact spot where we once spent the night.

But I don't. I told myself that I was going to talk to Callum, and as awful and awkward and terrifying as it is, I'm going to do it.

I trot up until I'm right at his side. "Hey," he says again, like he forgot that I was there in the first place.

"Callum," I say. "I saw you in the cemetery. With—with Fiona."

He sits down in the sand. "Yeah. I kinda thought you might have." He rubs the back of his neck and stares at the dirt.

"Yeah," I say. The only sound I hear is the chattering of

birds and the white noise of crashing waves. "Are you guys . . . I mean, are you two back together? Was I wrong about . . . about what I thought I saw?" *Please, please say yes. Say that I was wrong, that you were just comforting her because she got a bad grade or you were giving her a hug congratulating her on her new boyfriend that she's super in love with.*

"No," Callum says. "You weren't wrong."

Oh, I hadn't noticed that the knife in my stomach was also burning hot and covered in spikes. How unpleasant.

"But," he says, "we're not back together. I mean, yes. We were there. And we were flirting. And . . . we kissed a bit."

Did I say burning hot and covered in spikes? Silly me, I meant made of lasers that shock you on an atomic level.

"Oh," I say. It's all I can manage to get out.

"But it's not like that. I mean, yeah, me and Fiona had a thing, and she broke it off with me, but it's just sort of habit when the two of us are together. We're actually awful together. Complete rubbish. I didn't think anything was going to happen, I mean."

"Oh," I say again. I am the Oscar Wilde of monosyllables.

"I like you, Nora," he says finally.

"I like you too, Callum. I mean, I liked you."

"And I want to hang out with you and spend time with you and get to know you because you're cool and interesting and talented and have *excellent* taste in films." He grins as me, but the smile fades almost immediately. "But, y'know . . . you're leaving."

"I get it," I say. I don't get it. Is he breaking it off with me? Is he trying to say he wants to be with me while I'm here?

"And, y'know," he says, looking at his feet, "it's like I don't *really* know you or anything about you. Like, what do you like? What—I don't know—how many bones have you broken? Who are you?"

The answer: zero. Maybe I'm just as boring as he thinks I am. I begin mentally scrolling through my Rolodex of facts about myself that I use when teachers make us go around and name a fun fact about ourselves on the first day of school. *My name is Nora Parker-Holmes. My grandfather is Robert Parker—you know, the famous artist. I have a scar on the back of my wrist from trying to cook SpaghettiOs when I was four. I'm allergic to penicillin.* None of that seems very helpful.

"Well, no broken bones," I say when the silence goes on too long. "And I don't know. I don't think I know who I am either. I'm trying to come up with something, but I'm just getting, like, a list of facts about myself."

Callum puts his arm around me and pulls me tight to his body. "What am I going to do with you?" he says, and I can't tell whether he's being playful or serious, but his body touching my body reminds me just how much I want to be near him.

"Well," I say, letting my lips curl into the tiniest smile for the first time since I saw him, "I'm here for another week. We don't have to plan for anything longer or more complicated than that. You can try to get to know me."

"Live for the present, huh," Callum says, but he doesn't sound too certain.

"I never could get into *Lord of the Rings*, and maybe a week is just long enough for you to explain to me what's so good about it."

Callum smiles too, a shy, small smile, and then he begins laughing the same big laugh he had the night we first met. "I'll *barely* be able get you through *The Silmarillion* in a week!"

He curls both of his hands around my face and pulls me in, and we're kissing, and it feels amazing. I let all of my anxiety about Nick and Lena and my mother and my art career fade away, and I think only about how nice it is to have my fingers in Callum's hair and how tingly I get when he runs his hands across my thighs.

"Hey," he says, pulling away. "I'm taking you to Galway tomorrow."

"Is that so?"

"You and I are going to see the Cliffs of Moher. I would not be fulfilling my role as a romantic Irishman if I didn't take you. Plus, it's pretty much the greatest make-out spot in the world."

"It's a deal," I say, and this time I'm the one who pulls him in for a long kiss.

"K-I-S-S-I-N-G!" Tess sings as she bounds up the beach. Callum and I break apart, embarrassed.

"You guys make it into the lighthouse?" I ask.

"Boy wonder managed to spring the lock. Aaaaaaaand . . ." With a flourish, she pulls a handful of junk from behind her back. "The Kennedy Treasure. Told you it was real." She's holding a broken fishing rod, two empty potato chip bags, a scrap of a tire, and a beaten-up license plate. "Your share of the treasure," she says, passing me the license plate.

"The American government will never know what we know," I say. Tess and I both salute.

"You're not a little disappointed?" Rodger says, huffing, finally making it to us.

"Are you kidding?" Tess says. "A license plate and broken fishing rod are *way* better than the treasure of 'friendship.'"

"Oh, definitely," Callum says. "If there's one thing that's over-rated, it's the companionship of people who care about you."

"Good thing I hate all of you," Rodger says, but he's smiling while he says it.

23

PACKING FOR A day trip to the Cliffs of Moher, I've decided to bring:

- One (1) raincoat, because the weather app seems as indecisive as a girl getting dressed before a first date
- My sketchpad and three (3) freshly sharpened pencils
- Two (2) Toffee Crisp candy bars, which I will devour as often as I am able until I leave the country and then attempt to illegally smuggle back a lifetime supply to the United States
- A bestselling novel about a man struggling to make it on his own in New York City in this complicated post-9/11 world that the blurbs on the cover said was "compelling . . . groundbreaking prose and insight about the millennial psyche" and "the work of the next David

Foster Wallace" but that I have yet to be motivated to open. A four-hour bus ride both ways means now's the time to actually get through it.

- One (1) iPhone with which to take a humiliating amount of selfies to post to Instagram

It all fits inside a sleek black backpack that I've kept rolled in my main carry-on suitcase the entire trip for this exact purpose. Callum and I have agreed to meet at the bus stop at eight A.M.— just enough time, he said, for us to grab coffee at the shop on the corner and make it back with plenty of time for the eight twenty-four bus to Galway. "I'd drive us there, but Dad can't go all day without the truck," he said. "Also, parking is a fucking nightmare."

I go downstairs and find my mom cooking breakfast on the stove, with thick slices of Evelyn's homemade bread already in the toaster. "Your backpack on already? We're not leaving until this afternoon."

"What do you mean? I'm spending the weekend with Callum. In Galway."

My mom drops the spatula on the counter, and bits of scrambled egg fly into the air. "What? You didn't tell me that."

Oh shit. No, no, I definitely didn't. I really, really should have. I could've sworn . . . Nope. No. I didn't. "Oh god, I am *so* sorry. I've been so busy trying to finish this project for Declan and spending more time with Maeve and Tess . . . I totally forgot to mention it. *But*," I say, "in my defense, we do have that 'no more commentary on my life, more freedom because you're staying' thing?"

"Did you also forget," she says, "that we were going to go to Belfast this weekend?"

Double shit. Triple shit.

Option A: *Run. Run as fast as I can to the bus station, go to Galway, and live there forever. Change my name and begin a new life as Eimer the Shipbuilder.*

Option B: *Melt into liquid form and disappear in the floorboards.*

Option C: *Apologize profusely, and then apologize some more. Beg forgiveness, and then apologize again.*

"I am so sorry," I say. Option C it is. I contemplate getting on my knees, but I decide against it. "I totally forgot."

"Well, that's all right. Just make sure you message Callum before he makes too many plans." She returns to her eggs.

"Wait. I mean"—I struggle with choosing the right words—"I'm still planning on going with Callum. I mean, I want to go to Galway and . . . and see the Cliffs."

"So," she says, "you are bailing on the plans that you and I made to go off with a boy you barely know."

"Mom, I'm sorry. I'm not *bailing*. Yes, I want to go with Callum. I made a mistake, but this trip is still supposed to be about me gaining some freedom. Like you promised, remember?"

"I thought . . ." She pauses. "I thought that you would have wanted to spend *some* time with your mother. When you made plans with her. When she came halfway around the world to be with you. I mean, really, Nora, how selfish can you be?"

And that's when I lose it. "I never asked you to come!" I shout so loud that I'm probably waking Evelyn and half the town, but I don't care. I've kept what I've wanted to say inside for too long, and now that it's found a tiny hole to release the pressure, everything is coming out in full force. "You were never supposed to be here in the first place. And you were never supposed to stay this long! *I'm selfish? ME?* What about you? Crashing my trip and manipulating me into staying *even longer* than I originally agreed to? *Why* are you still here?"

My mother sits down at the kitchen table. I have never seen her respond to confrontation this way. The flame is still on underneath the pan of eggs. They're about to burn, but neither of us dares to move. "I lost my job, Nora."

The toaster dings.

I try to wrap my head around what she just said. "Because . . . because of this trip? Because you've been gone for so long?"

"No, Nora." I don't like the way she keeps repeating my name. "Before we left. I . . ." Her voice cracks. "Going back to work has been hard. I'm not as quick as I once was, or as I thought I would be, and they're bringing in younger partners, and with you, and things changing, I just . . . It was the Edwards case. I made a mistake. And with Walter—I mean, with your father gone . . . I thought taking some time to go on this trip would help me figure out what to do next."

"No," I say, synapses in my brain firing like an electrical storm. "Hold on. This happened *before* the trip? So this whole time—" My voice is sharper than it usually is, shriller. I don't quite recognize myself, but at this moment, the most important thing is that my mom keeps talking, that I make sense of what she's saying, because right now everything is just a blur.

She's hysterical now, hands shaking, hair frizzing at the temples. I haven't seen her like this since the day after Dad left, and I'm about to comfort her when a terrible thought creeps into my brain.

"At the airport, you told me—you said you wanted to come on this trip to 'get to know me.' I went along with it because I thought it was *nice*. I thought it was nice that my mother finally wanted to get to know me. But that's not why you came. You . . . lied?"

"What do you mean, Nora?"

"I mean"—my voice is getting louder—"I mean all of that stuff you said, at the airport and here, about wanting to get to know me before I leave for college, it was all bullshit. You came here for *you*. To clear *your* head? You lied to me and guilt-tripped me and *manipulated* me so that you could control me. You couldn't just let me have this one thing."

"You don't understand what you're saying," she says, standing up. She walks over and turns off the stove with a definitive click. "Do you think it was easy having a baby when I was twenty-two, relying on help from a father who wasn't sure when or if his next painting would ever sell? How hard it was to go back to work after your father left? I've been fighting to take care of myself my entire life.

"When I tell you to come up with a plan B, it's not because I don't think art is a *wonderful* pastime. It's because I want a daughter who's able to take care of herself and will never need to rely on anybody else for anything. It's because you're being naive and unrealistic."

Heart rate up, I shout back: "But I'm good enough! I got into the Deece!"

My mother laughs a bitter, terrible laugh. "You got into *the Deece* because your grandfather wrote you a letter of recommendation, Nora."

"He didn't even know I applied!" I spit back. "I sent an application with my portfolio, which you would know if you paid attention to anything that ever mattered to me. If you paid attention to anything other than your stupid job and stupid clothes and stupid exercise."

My mother looks at me, her eyes aiming for sympathy but landing on condescension. "Of course he knew, Nora. Who do you think told him to write the letter of recommendation?"

We look each other in the eye for the first time all morning. We're both breathing heavily, and my mom's eyes are watering.

I turn around and storm up to my room, stomping so hard with each step it's like I'm trying to transmit my rage and sadness into the floorboards. It doesn't work.

There are three unread messages from Callum on my phone: *"Hey, you on your way?" "Bus coming soon!!" "You still coming?"* I throw my phone as hard as I can onto my bed, where it bounces innocently on a pillow and lands on the floor. If I don't look at it, it doesn't exist.

I hear my mom leave the cottage, and I'm left alone, lying on my bed, closing my eyes, and pressing my palm against my forehead, where a throbbing headache is blooming, hoping that in a few minutes my head will hurt less and everything will be less complicated. The day is going on without me, and I am here: stagnant, frozen, crying. I stay immobile on my bed as the buzzing message notifications from my phone become more and more infrequent until, finally, they cease altogether.

24

IT'S STILL DAWN, and sunrise is just barely visible as I look out the taxi's rearview window. I wonder if Callum is awake yet, whether he's seen the note I left on the stoop of his dad's house. I tried to keep it from becoming too sappy, but I'm not sure I succeeded.

Dear Callum,

I'm really sorry for missing our trip to Galway. And the Cliffs of Moher. I didn't even get a chance to tell you how excited I was to quote *The Princess Bride* with you. I could go into detail about how complicated things got, but it's going to be easier for both of us if I say I ran into problems with my mom. And then I spent the rest of the day thinking about what I want and who I am (just some light, breezy things), and what I realized is that I need a chance to be on my own, completely. To experience what it's like to travel—and be an artist—on my own terms. So I changed my flight and left a little early for Florence—the next step on Grandpa's tour.

I've spent so long trying to be there for my mom, and holding my tongue around my best friend, and falling for boys who don't feel the same way about me that I forgot who I am without all of that. But I hope you know that this isn't about you. Really. It's about me: the cliché American girl in Europe trying to find herself.

So you might be wondering: Who *is* Nora Parker-Holmes? Excellent question. I've come up with the following lists.

Things I Hate:
- The color orange
- The smacking sound my mom's lips make before she's about to say something
- Boys with gauges in their ears
- Chalky fingers after using pastels
- Jazz music, the fast kind that makes me anxious
- The thin, pasty, flat strands that stick to a banana after you peel it

Things I Like:

- Brie cheese
- The ding from a text message
- Wearing a bathrobe after a shower
- Ginger tea
- Squeezing paint out of an aluminum tube
- Maybe you. Probably you. Definitely you.

There are a million more things I want to talk to you about (and a million more locations where I want to make out with you), but for right now, this is more important. I really, really hope I get to see you again. The miracle of the Internet means that, if you'll still have me after totally ditching you, we can video chat and you can teach me all about *Lord of the Rings* from across the Atlantic Ocean. Of course, there's also the distinct possibility that you'll get into Brown and I'll get into RISD, in which case, I'll see you in Rhode Island. And I'll buy your ticket to the next Marvel Cinematic Universe movie when we see it together to make up for ditching you.

Love,
Nora

P.S. If you're not too mad at me, check out Ophelia in Paradise. I drew something before I left that you might like.

* * *

"Going to the airport?" the taxi driver asks over her shoulder. "What terminal?"

"Ummmm." So this is what it feels like to be on your own. Responsible for all the annoying little things. I scramble to find my confirmation e-mail. "Aer Lingus," I say. "Terminal One." Already I feel more competent and capable.

There's one more letter I need to write before I can actually tell myself that I've taken control of my own life, but I won't be able to start it until I'm on the plane. In the time it took to wait in line at security, get scanned by those terrifying glass-box terrorism preventers, find the gate, board the plane, find my seat . . . I still haven't figured out how to start the first sentence. And so I just start the letter anyway with whatever's on my mind and hope the right words will come somewhere in the middle.

NORA PARKER-HOLMES
To: LennyLady41@gmail.com
Subject: Leaving Ireland

Dear Lena,

Well, I've left Ireland. I'm officially on my own now—completely Alice Parker-free. You feel very grown-up boarding a plane on your own, saying "excuse me" to people and pretending you're an important businesswoman traveling from Ireland to Florence on important art-related business. I needed to get away from my mom for a bit. I think I've realized something you've been telling me for a while: I can't fix her life, and I don't have to. Sometimes I just need to be the kid and let her deal with whatever's going on. Does it sound like I'm in an after-school special?

I guess what I've learned at the Deece, other than that the Irish accent is inhumanly attractive (and that people in Ireland treat JFK like the pope), is that being an artist is tough. I only ever really saw my grandpa's success, but I didn't realize how hard he had to work to get there, or how lucky he was, or how much he and my mom sacrificed along the way.

I still want to be an artist, I think, but at least now I know that it's going to take more than an application to RISD and faith that everything will work out. The more I think about it, the more I like your plan of going to college and seeing what you like and going from there.

Yes (I know you were going to ask), I had to leave Callum, but the important thing for me right now is learning how to be okay without taking care of someone else or having someone else there to take care of me.

And I have something to tell you that I didn't tell you because I was embarrassed or hurt or a combination of both of those. I lost my virginity over winter break to Nick. And then he never texted me again, and I forgot about things until you started dating him in the spring, and I was too shocked or embarrassed or hurt or a combination of all of those to tell you. And then I waited too long, and I assumed you would hate me. Please don't hate me.

Love you forever,
Nora

For whatever reason, once I press send, I feel more alone than ever before. I finalized things with Callum and Lena, and I can't talk to my mother right now. It's just me and the flight attendant who looked at my pityingly when she saw that I was traveling alone.

Even though I totally try, I still can't get into the book I brought. The words just won't fix themselves into sentences that make sense. I alternate between sketching figures that come out looking disproportionately top-heavy and listening to the pilot's channel on the built-in radio.

I force myself not to check my e-mail to see if Lena responded until I'm at the hostel. The directions I printed to get me to the Ciao Hostel via public transportation said that I should buy a five-dollar bus ticket to the center of town and then take the number 4 bus from there, which doesn't sound too complicated until I get to the arrivals area of the airport and see that there are about five thousand buses and services claiming to go to the center of town, and another six thousand saying they're the number 4 bus. Apparently there are buses called ATAF and buses called LI-NEA, and according to something I read back home, I'm definitely supposed to use one of them, and I'm *definitely* supposed to avoid the other.

I see people waiting in line at a kiosk. *Am I also supposed to be waiting at that kiosk?* I'm not entirely sure what people are waiting in line for. Okay. I'm not a grouchy dad in a hacky road trip comedy. I can ask for directions. Before I pick the person to ask, a man with a mustache approaches me.

"Need a taxi?" he says in English.

"No, thank you," I say.

"No charge!" he says and makes an attempt to grab my carry-on for me and put it into his already popped car, which is black but otherwise gives no indication of being an actual taxi. I snatch my carry-on back. "No," I say. And just in case it doesn't translate, I waggle my finger. "No, no." He raises both hands and lowers his head apologetically, and I walk off as quickly as I can.

I wish I spoke Italian; if I spoke Italian, I would have stepped off the plane like I'm in a *Vanity Fair* photo shoot, with a white capelet and sunglasses and a hat. And I would have had a friend come pick me up in a tiny car—or no, on a moped— and I'd kiss her on both cheeks, and she'd toss me a helmet that I'd catch effortlessly, and we'd zip through the city, making everyone who saw us so jealous that they spit in the dirt.

I see a policewoman! She's smoking and she looks like she's off duty, but I need help, and a policewoman is the perfect person for a minor in a foreign country to talk to. I feel like they probably showed us a video about this sometime in elementary school.

"Please, *por favor*"—oh god, that's Spanish. Retreat to English. "Can you . . . help me, please?"

"I speak English," she says.

"Oh, thank god. I'm trying to get . . ." I shove my phone in her hand, the screen showing a map with a pin in my hostel's location. She zooms in.

"Ah," she says and points to one of the lines that I had about a one-in-five chance of choosing if she didn't help me. "Fine Austostrada A11. Buy the ticket here, and stop off at Via Rosselli 66. Two-minute walk from there."

"Ah! Thank you! Thank you," I say and begin rolling my bag off toward the right area, repeating the name of the bus and the stop in my head so I won't forget it.

"Very brave," she calls after me. Which makes me slightly nervous that the policewoman thinks it's brave to take a bus to where I'll be staying, because now I'm starting to think that the Florence bus system is a *Hunger Games*-style competition to the death. "Traveling on your own," she adds.

"Oh," I say. "Thanks."

She's already back to her cigarette.

I make it to the hostel after a few false turns and after cutting through what was almost definitely private property. The girl at the front desk gives me a thin, knobby towel and two keys—one for my room (which I'll share with thirteen strangers) and one for the locker under my bed, where I should keep my things.

Once I'm set up on my bed, I run out of excuses not to check Lena's e-mail. What, exactly, am I hoping she'll say? Something perfect and understanding like:

Nor—

I've never broken up with anyone faster in my whole life. He was a dillweed anyway. I bought the funfetti cake mix for the "We Hate Nick DiBasilio" party as soon as you get back.

You couldn't stop me from being your friend if you tried.

Xo,
Lenny

PS I'm so proud of you for staking out on your own. You need some space from Alice, and I'm sure she'll understand. I bet Callum will understand too.

PPS Get some gelato for me.

Refreshing, refreshing, refreshing, and . . . nothing. No new e-mails, except a coupon from Bed Bath and Beyond. Radio silence from my best friend in the world, to whom I just poured my heart out and who's probably going to hate me forever and abandon me to go off and join a clique with Nick's friends.

"Hard getting here?" the girl asks from behind the front desk.

"Kinda hard," I say back.

"Yeah, those trains can be rough," she replies. "Jelly Baby?" She hands me a bag of candies so strange that for the moment I forget all about Lena and my mom and Callum because, as it turns out, Jelly Babies are like giant gummy bears shaped like naked toddlers. And biting the head off a naked toddler right now feels better than I want to admit.

25

ONE OF THE benefits of being on my own is that no one can judge me for having an enormous cone of *one-scoop-raspberry-I-mean*-lampone-*and-one-scoop-hazelnut-please* gelato at eleven fifteen in the morning. It's practically yogurt, I tell myself: dairy, fruit, *nuts*. It's part of a healthy breakfast—every food group represented. I try not to let it drip on the paper from Grandpa, partly because I need to see the address but mostly because I don't want a single ounce of the most delicious thing I have ever eaten to go to waste.

Every part of Florence looks like it should be on a post-card. Even the cheap corner shops with crumbling bricks and primary-colored awnings that are literally *selling* postcards are picturesque. I could spend hours walking these streets, weaving between people and dipping into churches that look unassuming from the outside and then take your breath away the moment you're past the threshold: dark, ornate, baroque caverns with ceilings painted so beautifully it makes you want to cry; gilded altarpieces that seem like they shouldn't be allowed to have been hidden in this church that I might have just walked by without a second thought.

According to my travel guide, there's a "moderately priced classic Italian spot for lunch" just around the corner from the last church I dipped into. Once I spot the restaurant, the tiny AIR CONDITIONING! sign in the window is all I need to convince me that I've chosen the right place. My dress is sticking to the back of my thighs, and I can feel beads of sweat rolling down my sports bra. It's not just that Florence is hot; it's as if the sun has decided to be a tourist here too, weaving among the impossibly dense crowds with its heat and light, trying to be unobtrusive but failing. *Pardon me, excuse me, four-hundred-thirty-thousand-mile dwarf star here trying to get through to the Uffizi Gallery.*

I see the words "mushroom" and "prosciutto" and "pizza" together, and my mind is made up. "*Funghi e prosciutto pizza,* please," I say, realizing too late that I definitely cannot speak Italian and I'm just embarrassing myself in trying. The waiter nods and leaves me at the table, alone, in Florence, at two P.M. on a Monday afternoon.

Look at me! I'm in a foreign city, eating lunch at a restaurant by myself. This is the sort of *Eat Pray Love* magic that most people dream of. And I'm achieving it! With my sunglasses perched on my head, I probably look like Audrey Hepburn. I bet everyone else in the restaurant is whispering to one another:

"Who *is* that girl? So young!"

"Is she traveling alone?"

"Must be *American*."

"So glamorous!"

The pizza is taking a little while to make it to my table, and I forgot to bring a book, so I just sort of thumb through my travel guide, rereading passages I already memorized.

When my pizza still hasn't arrived, the imaginary conversations in my head change a bit:

"Is she eating all alone?"

"So sad!"

"I bet even if a boy liked her, she'd abandon him and basically force him into the arms of his redheaded ex."

"Or maybe a hot blonde Australian girl who was also at an artists' colony with her! I bet this boy would have been pretty flirty with a hot blonde Australian girl."

"What prescient strangers we are!"

Rather than listen to these imaginary strangers, who seem to have turned against me, I open the envelope from Grandpa. To my surprise, only a small scrap of paper falls out this time, a square neatly cut from a notebook.

JUST ONE GALLERY: VIA DEL MORO 24

Before I can consider it fully, the pizza comes out hot, with bubbling cheese and mushrooms so flavorful and earthy that I make a pact with myself never to eat anything but pizza in Florence again. Food is ruined for me. I will eat nothing but pizza here until I die. This isn't American pizza, the Domino's stuff with a doughy crust that tastes a bit too much like a dried dish sponge and cheese like salty plastic. This is a revelation. Maybe that's why Grandpa didn't give me an assignment in Florence: He knew nothing I painted could hope to compete with the pizza here.

"Wait," I shout at a waiter, who seems surprisingly okay with having a strange American yelling at him. "Do you have WiFi here?"

Without a word, the waiter disappears and reemerges from the back with a tiny slip of paper with a string of numbers: a password.

Sweet, merciful god. I click the network name and type the random letters of a password and then watch the swirling loading sign until—YES—full WiFi strength.

I click on my e-mail. Still nothing from Lena. She couldn't even reply with a "Sorry" or a "Sucks to be you" or a succinct "THIS FRIENDSHIP IS OVER."

And the pizza is gone. All I can do is scroll impotently through my phone and try to waste a few more minutes before I go back out into the Florentine heat.

And then I see it: the tiny red exclamation point in the outbox of my Gmail account. My e-mail to Lena didn't send! And why did I think it would? I was in a taxi in rural Ireland with no data! My heart catches in my chest, and I'm not sure whether it's relief or disappointment or something in between. I feel like I made a suicide jump off the Golden Gate Bridge and got caught in a filament-thin net.

I look around as if there's going to be a sign somewhere in the restaurant that says: SEND IT NOW THAT YOU HAVE WIFI! or one that says: DELETE IT, YOU FOOL! Instead, all I get is a plain brick wall and a waitstaff getting bored near the kitchen.

I take a deep breath. And then another.

I don't send the e-mail.

This trip is about me and my art and my assignments for Grandpa. I don't want to relive the past twenty-four hours of refreshing my e-mail every time I have access to WiFi.

And then a text pops up from Lena. And then another. And then another, accumulated in the time my phone wasn't taking messages.

NORA
NORA
FUCK THIS
FUCK EVERYTHING
HE'S BEEN CHEATING ON ME
NICK
I KNOW YOU'RE OFF IN EUROPE, BUT HE HAS HOOKED
UP WITH HALF OF THE VARSITY SOCCER TEAM SINCE WE
STARTED DATING
OBVIOUSLY BROKE UP
UFDJDFFDJDFJDJDJK

The text I write back comes so easily compared to the tortured letter I almost sent: *Lenny—he was an asshole. Trust me, I know. You can do so much better. I can't give you all the love you need while I'm away, but I'm coming home soon, and I'll bring the funfetti cake mix for our I Hate Nick DiBasilio Party.*

It wasn't karma. Friends never deserve that. But what Lena and I did need were these reasons to fall back into each other's arms, these mutual understandings about the boys who broke our hearts and whose tiny betrayals will grow tinier and tinier in the rearview mirror.

I pay the bill with leftover euros from Ireland (how amazing and weird that a plane ride and countries away, the money is still the same), and I begin walking toward the gallery, following the map in the back of the guidebook.

The gallery is small, a white building with big glass windows. It took me a few times walking up and down the street to actually spot it, since the gallery name was covered with creeping ivy. It looks more like a schoolhouse than an art gallery, or maybe an alternative-style church, the type where the priest plays acoustic guitar.

Stepping inside the building, a whoosh of air conditioning descends over me. Coming from the hot street, it's like entering a cold pool. I'm instantly embarrassed about what I'm wearing: leggings that I haven't washed in two weeks and a T-shirt that may or may not have a chocolate stain near the shoulder. I'm sweaty from walking, and my mouth is sticky with pizza residue; I don't even want to think about what my hair must look like after the plane-bus-bunk-bed day I had yesterday.

But then I see a pamphlet on the counter by the door, and I forget all of that: It's a Robert Parker show, and the pamphlet shows a picture of Grandpa in black and white, his head slightly tilted, caught mid-laugh.

I haven't seen any of these paintings before. I've been so busy worrying about college applications and boys and my mom that I haven't painted with Grandpa in months. The paintings are gorgeous—confident brushstrokes and scenes that stay in your mind even after your eyes leave the canvas, after you go about your day. I recognize one landscape as the view out of his kitchen window; another scene depicts a young girl who looks like she might once have been my mom, smiling from the floor where she's watching TV on her stomach.

There are so many people crowding around one work in the back of the gallery that even though it seems to take up half the wall, I can't actually make out what it is. I wait while a few people shuffle past, and then I elbow my way toward the front of the group. I can only see the title of the work, on a small burnished bronze placard.

THE NEW READER AND THE WATCHER
ROBERT PARKER AND NORA PARKER-HOLMES
MIXED MEDIA

It's a reproduction of his most famous painting, *The Reader and the Watcher*. The living room is the same: the sagging vintage sofa, the suggestion of light coming from the kitchen, the wide window on the right side of the room.

But the figures are different. They're versions of the figures in his original painting—the girl reading, the man looking out the window with a cigarette in his hand—but the drawings are mine. They're the cartoon versions I created and posted on my Tumblr. Grandpa painted the background in a realistic style and then interposed my two-dimensional characters in the scene.

It looks incredible. It's my favorite painting in the world.

". . . more whimsical than we've seen in Parker's career," I hear someone say.

". . . new artistic voice . . ."

". . . a statement on the merging of commerce and art . . . Internet culture . . . youth."

"I think it's the best thing he's ever done."

I recognize the last voice. I turn and see my mom, Alice Parker, standing in a gallery in Florence with tears in her eyes. "It's wonderful, isn't it?" she says.

I forget about the painting, I forget about Lena, I forget about Callum.

"Mom?"

She takes one step forward, hesitant, not sure what terms we left on. I don't think I really know what terms we left on either. I was furious with her when I got into the cab to go to the airport, ready to legally emancipate myself from the Parker side of my hyphenated last name. But seeing her, here, in Florence, after two days of wandering alone, all I want to do is hug her. But I don't. Instead I ask, "How did you get here?"

She laughs a little. "Your grandfather told me that if I didn't come to this gallery in Florence, I would—what was the phrase he used?—ah, yes. 'Regret it for as long as I was your mother.'"

I don't know what to say. And so I just stand next to her and look back at the painting, the figures I drew, on a canvas, in a real gallery. We stand there together for a while.

"It's wonderful," she says finally.

"Grandpa painted it," I say, not making eye contact. Grandpa was the one who got me into the Deece, and he's the one who got me into this gallery. A small part of me, a part gnawing away at me, knows that.

"Nora," my mom says, "look at me." I do. And I see that she's almost crying, the corners of her eyes going blurry. She's not wearing lipstick, and she looks younger than she has in years. "Your grandfather is wonderful. And he has been a tremendous help. But it's what you've done with it that makes me proud of you."

"He got me into the Deece," I say, my eyes beginning to tear.

The corners of her mouth tighten, and she puts a hand on my shoulder. "Okay," she says. "He wrote a letter. Do you know how much guts it took for you to *apply* to this artists' colony in the first place? To seek it out? To want to go? To make a decision to travel around the world by yourself? You could get into every prestigious artists' colony in the country and do you know what I'd be proud of?"

I shake my head.

"I would be proud," my mom says, "of who you are. And," she adds, "of who you want to be. And all the mistakes you're going to make. And all the wonderful successes you're going to have."

And with that, I am hugging my mom, and I'm so grateful that she's here to share this with me—my first piece in an art gallery.

"I'm sorry," I say into her shoulder. "I should have been better. I mean, more understanding. With the job stuff . . . I'm sorry."

"Nora," my mom says, pulling away with one hand on each shoulder. I'm three inches taller than her, but she seems bigger than she ever has. "Listen to me. My job and my life are not your concern. All you need to worry about is picking a college you love and figuring out what makes you happy. Do you hear me?"

I nod.

"I'm going to find a new job," she says. "I'm going to be just fine." She holds my hand and turns to look at the painting again. "I just love that style. I'm so glad the artist has an entire blog where she posts things she's done."

"You've seen my Tumblr?"

She laughs a little. "Yes, Miss Ophelia in Paradise. Your mother figured out how to find a blog. Although I have to say, I'm not sure I understand the most recent post?" She pulls out her phone and scrolls to a page that she has book-marked. "It's a superhero, right? 'The Silmarillionaire'? I've never heard of him."

Now I'm laughing, and everyone else in the gallery is looking over at us, not because we're being loud, obnoxious Americans, but because we're having more fun than anyone else. "It's a superhero I made up," I say. "His powers are all *Lord of the Rings*-themed."

"He looks familiar," my mom says, zooming in on the face. "He's not from anything else?"

"Well," I say, looking at the floor and trying to suppress a smile, "his secret identity is Callum Cassidy."

"Ah," she says. And we just stay holding hands, walking through the gallery, spending an equal amount of time looking at Grandpa's new paintings and looking at the faces of other people looking.

"You should go back," my mom says finally, when we've made our way out of the gallery. "To Ireland, I mean. Be with Callum and your friends. Spend more time at the Deece. Finish out your program."

I think about it. I imagine going back to the DCYA and seeing Callum again, the way he'd pick me up and spin me around the minute I arrived, like I weighed nothing and he just wanted his arms around as much of me as possible. I imagine the two of us going to the Cliffs of Moher. And making out there. I imagine painting with Maeve and asking her to teach me how she's *so good* at carving plates. I want to ask Rodger to bring me to the lighthouse so I can actually see what's inside.

"I don't think I'm going to go back," I say. My mom looks taken aback; her mouth hangs open slightly, as if she's tempted to say something, but she doesn't. "At least not now. The last stop on Grandpa's trip for me was London. I've never been, and I want to see it while I have the chance. Even if it means being on my own for a little bit."

My mom hugs me. She smells like detergent and airplane seats and Evelyn's bread. "I'm so proud of you," she says into my ear. "Not because of your paintings, or your blog, or because of what you do, but because of who you are."

"I love you too."

In a few days, I'll be leaving Florence with a carry-on suit-case that's exactly twenty inches long and filled with dirty clothes and half-used art supplies, a sketch of a waitress in a Parisian café and a drawing of the uneven Brussels town hall to bring back to Grandpa, a bent Irish license plate, and a tattered copy of *The Silmarillion*. But while I'm in Florence, I'm going to see as much as I possibly can.

My mom squeezes my hand. "How about you and I get some gelato?"

I absolutely do not tell her that I ate gelato an hour and a half ago. "I know a great place."

"Already? You've been here half a day!"

"I'm an experienced traveler."

Before we leave the gallery, I grab one of the pamphlets by the door: just one more thing to add to my suitcase.

My mother and I head out into the heat of Florence, buoyed by everything that happened to us and the possibilities of what there's still left to do.

EPILOGUE

GRANDPA'S ASSIGNMENT PACKET for London is heavier than any of the others. I hadn't really noticed how much it weighed when it had been at the bottom of my carry-on the entire trip. But now, on the plane to London, I feel as though it's as good a time as any to finally open it: my last assignment from Grandpa. A slim leather-bound notebook falls out of the envelope, along with a letter.

CONGRATULATIONS. YOU ARE OFFICIALLY A GALLERY-EXHIBITED PROFESSIONAL ARTIST. OF COURSE, PROPER DECORUM USUALLY INVOLVES INFORMING THE ARTIST BEFORE THE WORK IS HUNG, BUT I FELT IN THIS CASE A SURPRISE MIGHT BE WORTHY OF AN EXCEPTION.

PERHAPS I SHOULD ALSO LET YOU KNOW THAT
OUR WORK HAS ALREADY BEEN PURCHASED
BY A COLLECTOR WITH A SERIOUS EYE, FOR A
CONSIDERABLE SUM. I'VE TAKEN THE LIBERTY
OF DEPOSITING YOUR PERCENTAGE INTO YOUR
COLLEGE SAVINGS ACCOUNT, AND THEN TAKEN
THE LIBERTY OF DEPOSITING MY PERCENTAGE
INTO YOUR COLLEGE SAVINGS ACCOUNT. AFTER
ALL, AS ANYONE WHO SAW THE EXHIBITION
WOULD ATTEST, IT IS TRULY YOUR UNIQUE
STYLE THAT MAKES THE PIECE.

AS FOR YOUR FINAL ASSIGNMENT: SEE LONDON.
ENJOY THE CITY. TAKE THE ENCLOSED
NOTEBOOK AND FILL IT AS YOU SEE FIT. I
RECOMMEND THE WALLACE GALLERY AND THE
TATE MODERN. SKETCH EVERYTHING YOU SEE
AND EVERYTHING YOU DREAM. YOU ARE AN
ARIST, MY DARLING, AND THE WORLD DESERVES
TO SEE HOW YOU SEE THE WORLD.

BECOMING AN ARTIST IS A RECKLESS ACT OF
INSANITY. BUT, IF I MAY QUOTE A PLAY THAT
I THINK MIGHT BE A FAVORITE OF YOURS,
"THOUGH THIS BE MADNESS, / YET THERE IS
METHOD IN'T."

LEARN THE METHODS, AND THEN ENJOY THE
MADNESS.

I LOVE YOU.

—RP

ACKNOWLEDGMENTS

Thank you so much to Marissa Grossman, Ben Schrank, and the entire team at Razorbill for their faith in me and for the vision for this book that allowed it to become a reality.

I couldn't have done this without my agent, Dan Mandel, who believed in me when I was an overeager, under-prepared college kid, and who has been with me every step of the way—through panicked phone calls and panicked e-mails.

To Drew and Vinnie at the *Observer* for all of their help and support while I was holding a job and also trying to make a book.

To Maddi, because I couldn't have had a better traveling companion when I went on my trip to Europe.

To Rory, Claire, Cameron, and Jono for letting me use the gang, a little bit, in this book.

To the girls in the dressing room during the 2015 Brown University production of *Sweeney Todd*, who believed I could be a success before anyone else, and to whom I promised a dedication in my first book.

To Matt, for being there for me.

And to Mom, Dad, Zach, Caroline, and Hallie. I love you so much, and I'll never be able to thank you enough for all of the support I get from you. The only reason I'm able to write books in New York is because I know I have a safe place to fall.